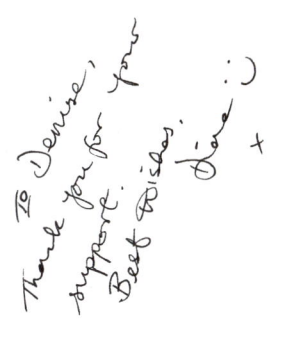

REFLECTIONS

A collection of stories and poems

By Diane West

Reflections © Diane West 2017.

All rights reserved. The author asserts their moral right under the Copyright, Designs and Patents Act 1988 to be identified as the author of this work.

Published by The Solopreneur Publishing Company Ltd,
West Yorkshire WF9 1PB
www.thesolopreneur.co.uk

Except for the quotation of small passages for the purposes of criticism and review, no part of this publication may be reproduced, stored in a retrieval system, or transmitted, in any form or by any means, electronic, mechanical, photocopying, recording or otherwise, except under the terms of the Copyright, Designs and Patents Act 1988 without the prior consent of the publisher at the address above.

The Solopreneur Publishing Company Ltd focuses on the needs of each individual author client. This book has been published through their 'Solopreneur Self-Publishing (SSP)' brand that enables authors to have complete control over their finished book whilst utilising the expert advice and services usually reserved for traditionally published print, in order to produce an attractive, engaging, quality product. Please note, however, that final editorial decisions and approval rested with the author. The publisher takes no responsibility for the accuracy of the content.

ISBN – 978-0-9957520-2-3

Printed in the U.K.

Dedication

This book is dedicated in memory of my mother, who lost her battle to Cancer in April 2016. If I am half the woman she was, then I am proud of myself.

'Right you are then'.

Contents

About the author

Mother Love (poem) dedicated to my mum	1
Naked in my grief (poem)	2
Retail Therapy (story)	3
Dandelions, Buttercups, and Daisy (story)	12
Good Old Graffiti (story)	25
No Explanation (story)	30
Simply Blue (story)	56
Crying Shame – Part One and Part Two (story)	86
Crying Shame (poem)	122
Over the hill (poem)	123
Ode to dieting (poem)	125
Ode to my left foot (poem)	126
Stupid O'clock (poem)	127
Tick Tock Mind Clock (poem)	128
A one day pass to heaven (poem) dedicated to my son Karl.	129
Melancholy Dream (poem)	130
In Nature's Hands (poem)	131
The candle of life (poem)	133
Life after death (poem)	135
The Meaning of Life (poem)	136
Burlesque (poem)	137
The Last Soldier (poem)	138
Lady of the night! (poem)	139
From Kings and Queens (poem)	141
My Forever Friend (poem) dedicated to my friend Kay.	143
Sleeping with the light on (Prologue)	144

About the author

They say you can tell a lot about someone by what they write.

I have been writing since I was a young girl. My love of writing began after first reading the book 'To Kill a Mocking Bird' by Harper Lee. This was given to me by my dad when I was nine. I didn't understand what it was about initially, but read it again at twelve years old. I loved how well it was written and how it transported me to an imaginary place. I knew then I wanted to write and transport an audience in the same way. Thus began my love affair with words. I entered a competition at the local library and although I didn't win, it spurred me on. I continued to write long after I married at sixteen, keeping diaries and writing secret stories and poems, which only I was privy to.

I became a mum, but tragically my son died suddenly as a baby. I went on to have four daughters, which kept me very busy. In my thirties I used poems as part of my GCSE exam submission, followed by an 'A' level in English, and an editing and proofreading course, all the time writing when possible. I worked for a local newspaper as a columnist for five years, which enabled me to gain more experience. I had various jobs over the years, gaining ideas from my experiences. Some of my stories and poems are a mixture of real experiences and fiction combined. I like to add a twist whenever I can and include humour. 'Good Old Graffiti' is based on my experiences at Upton Middle School. 'A One Day Pass to Heaven' I wrote for my son. Some other stories or poems included are drawn from personal events. I'll leave you as the reader to guess which ones.

In 2015, my mum was diagnosed with terminal lung cancer. Our family was devastated. We spent as much time as we could with her. My mum talked about my writing, and she told me she wished she had read more of it. She told me to follow my dream and publish a book. She died on April 23rd, 2016. I vowed to finish my first book and dedicate it to her and with my husband's encouragement I did. The first two poems are for her. The first one 'Mother Love' is in recognition of all that she was and all that she remains within my heart. The second poem 'Naked in my grief' is about my feelings after she is gone and coming to terms with her loss.

If she was as proud of me as I am of her, I have succeeded.

Mother Love

There is no love like Mother Love
Unconditional and given free
I saw it radiate from her eyes
Each time she looked at me

When she held me in her loving arms
My head against her breast
I felt her breath and beating heart
Felt safe within her nest

Her gentle ways would reassure
And chase away my fears
Her soft embrace and comforting kiss
Would wash away my tears

Through good and bad her love was strong
It's power never wavered
And every moment that we shared
I coveted and savoured

My memories will never fade
My love will never die
Your Mother Love is always here
To hold me when I cry

I love you now, I loved you then
My love for you so strong
I know your love is there for me
Long after you are gone

For Mother Love can never die
It lasts the test of time
And I'll keep it dear, forever here
In this beating heart of mine

Naked in my grief

A painted smile, I hide my pain, on the outside I look fine
But behind the mask, it's hidden deep, inside this heart of mine
It feels as if there is no air, left in my lungs to breathe
And what's the point of getting dressed, I feel naked in my grief.

I close my eyes to sleep each night, my mind is craving dream
Where once again I see you there, as real as ever you seem
On the surface though, it all seems fine, it's what's lurking underneath
When no matter how my armour wears, I'm still naked in my grief

My heart is heavy, my legs feel weak, and my mind just won't stay still
I can't relax, I don't belong, and I fear I never will
I long for peace and solitude, but I know there's no relief
My layers are never thick enough, for I'm naked in my grief

And though I try to shake it off and lift my head up high
I cannot fight the waterfall of silent tears I cry
And there's no point shaking this heart that's breaking or trying to have belief
All the pain that's there will be lying bare, as I'm naked in my grief

So if you see the hollowness when you look into my eyes
Remember that I'm not myself and it won't come as a surprise
For I feel the thorns of sorrow still and my necklace is a wreath
Just let me be, to sooth myself while I'm naked in my grief

Retail Therapy

There's nothing like a bit of retail therapy to make a person feel better.

That's the main reason I got into this business. I enjoyed making people happy. A satisfied customer gives me a bigger buzz than drugs or alcohol...not that I've tried drugs you understand, but I've had my share of the drink. I've over done it more than once too. There's nothing nice about having a nasty hangover the next day, or in my case the next two days. I never could drink very well. No, retail therapy is a much better way to enjoy yourself. I've been doing this job for almost four years now and never had a single complaint until yesterday that is.

The day started like any other day. I got up early to see my husband Mick off to work. He works abroad a lot, and he was leaving for an early flight to Washington. I hated it when he went away. He could be gone for weeks at a time, and I would count the days down until his return. Although he was going away to work, he always asked me if I'd like to go with him, but I had my own business to take care of. I couldn't afford to go flying off somewhere for weeks on end. I'd lose custom. No, I had a living to earn too. Besides, if I wasn't here to look after the house and keep the gardens nice it would all start looking a mess and then what would the neighbours think. We are lucky to be able to live in such a nice area, and it took us years to afford a house like this. In fact, if it wasn't for the extra income I bring in, we would still be struggling with a huge mortgage.

Anyway, I got him a clean shirt out and hung it over the chair for him then I went to make him a cup of coffee while he shaved and got dressed. When he came down, I was already sitting at the table reading the paper. Mick sat down opposite me, drank his coffee and had a quick read of the paper after I'd finished with it. Half an hour later he kissed me goodbye, and

I watched him drive away. I waved after him and blew him a kiss, as I always do when he leaves for work, then went back inside to get dressed.

I was upstairs trying to decide what colour underwear to put on when I heard a knock at the door. This was followed quickly by a loud banging. All I had on was a pair of pants, so I grabbed my dressing gown and quickly tied it round me. Another loud knock crashed down on my door and I tried to run down the stairs.

"Hang on" I shouted "I'm on my way. Just a minute please."

By now I had reached the front door and I pulled it open. Standing in front of the step were three policemen. Two faces I'd never seen before and the third a local PC who I'd met a few times.

"Good morning Mrs. Dexter," one of the younger officers said, "we'd like to have a word with you if that's possible. Can we come in please?"

Very polite they were, so of course, I invited them in.

"Come inside. Would you like a cup of tea or coffee? How can I help you?"

They followed me into the house and one of them closed the front door behind him. They told me they didn't want a drink, but thanked me for asking, so I took them straight into the living room. Two of them sat down on the sofa and the other, older officer sat in one of the chairs. I remained standing. I was in my dressing gown you see, and I knew if I sat down it would ride up, and as I was only wearing pants underneath, I didn't think it was a good idea.

"You have a lovely house Mrs. Dexter and in a very nice area," he smiled at me, and I felt just a little bit uncomfortable.

"Thank you, "I replied. "We're very lucky to be able to afford such a place, but then we do both work long hours to pay for it."

I had the strangest feeling this conversation was leading somewhere other than the nice area we live in.

I was right.

"I won't beat about the bush," said one of the young officers "we've had a serious complaint that you are running a brothel from these premises. That you are having people visit your home for sexual services."

Well, you should have seen my face. I didn't know whether to laugh or cry I just stood there with my mouth open. What a shock.

"Do you have anything to say about the accusation Mrs. Dexter? Are you running a sexual business from your premises?"

I denied it of course. What did they take me for? I was suddenly angry. Here I was earning my living and paying taxes like everyone else. This was uncalled for.

"I'm sorry officer, but I'm in shock. I can't believe anyone would do such a thing? Who would waste your time and mine with such an absurd accusation? Can you tell me who made this silly claim? Was it my neighbours? Who?"

"Calm down Mrs. Dexter, no point in getting all upset. It's just a routine call. When we get complaints like this, we have to follow them up. It would help if we could take a look around the premises if you don't mind that is?"

The Policeman who spoke to me put his arm on my shoulder as if to reassure me.

"No, of course I don't mind. I have nothing to hide."

I took them into the kitchen first then I showed them into the dining room and then the conservatory. Piled high in the corner were lots of brown boxes.

"Would you like to see inside the boxes? I run a business from home and all my stock is inside."

They all shook their heads.

"No love it's fine," one of them replied. "The boxes don't concern us. If we could just have a look upstairs and then we'll be on our way."

I smiled and nodded. I led the way, and they followed behind me. I showed them the family bathroom first.

After a quick peep around the door, I took them into the bedrooms, one by one. Finally, I showed them the guest room. Their eyes nearly popped out of their heads. The room was full of lingerie, sexy underwear of every colour. On the bed, there were whips, masks, vibrators, corsets, basques and high heel rubber boots. Not to mention the tubes of oils and flavoured condoms scattered on the bedside table. It was like Aladdin's cave to them. Their faces were a picture. Before I had a chance to explain, the older Policeman turned to me and said:

"Can you tell me what this is all about Mrs. Dexter? You had better have a good reason for all this."

Try as I might, I couldn't keep the smirk on my face from spreading into a massive grin and then a laugh.

"I'm sorry gentlemen. Please forgive me for laughing, but you had to be where I'm standing and see your face, 'Sweet Hunny'...that's what this is all about. I work for them as a representative. I sell their products from home and do party plans. No doubt you've heard of Ann Summers, well this is a similar type of company. The boxes downstairs are full of ordered stock. I can show you the invoices and even go on the website if you like. You can see for yourselves then."

"Er...no need for that Mrs. Dexter. I'm sure we're quite happy with the explanation you've given us. We're sorry to have troubled you, but you understand we have a job to do and we have to be seen to be doing it properly. If you'd kindly see us out, we'll be on our way and leave you to your, erm' work."

The other two officers were smirking by now, and I could see they found the whole situation extremely amusing. I escorted them all downstairs and saw them out of the front door. I watched them walk up the path and, as they drove away, I stole a quick look at my watch.

"Bugger, look at the time. I'm not dressed, and I've got a customer in fifteen minutes."

I ran up the stairs, almost leaping the steps and hastily got myself dressed and organised. I'd just finished cleaning my teeth when the doorbell went.

"Perfect timing," I thought, as I dashed downstairs to open the door.

"Hello, Tommy. Wow, you look smart today. Come in."

I let him in and closed the door behind him, making sure the latch was dropped.

"Go on up," I told him "you know the routine by now. So what'll it be today, Dominatrix or French Maid? Your choice!"

Dandelions, Buttercups, and Daisy

"One o'clock, two o'clock, three o'clock, four," she repeated the rhyme over and over again in her head, trying to remember the rest of it.

"One o'clock, two o'clock," thud.

The first blow rained down on her face, with a second following quickly. She tried not to scream and bit her bottom lip so hard her tooth cut the inside of it. Before she had chance to stop him, David had grabbed a hand full of hair and was dragging her head backwards. Her body followed automatically as if sensing any delay would result in half her scalp being torn away. Not an easy thing to do, getting up backwards from a lying position on your stomach. Daisy knew trying to resist would only make David angrier, so she did what she thought he wanted her to do. No sooner was she on her feet, than he knocked her down again with a sharp kick to the back of her knees. This time she did scream and loudly. Her legs crumpled to the floor, and she landed in a heap, sobbing.

"That hurt. Oh god that hurt so much," she thought.

The dandelion she'd been holding was crushed when her hand hit the ground. She had picked it up earlier and was blowing it, just as she used to when she was a little girl. This was how you told the time with a dandelion clock. As the fluff segments left the flower, she would count; one o'clock, two o'clock, three o'clock, four o'clock and so on. The number she arrived at when all the fluff was gone, would tell her what time it was. It was a game that all Daisy's friends played when they were children. There was a rhyme they used to sing, and as she tried to blot out the pain, she tried to recall it in her head again, but all she could think of was her throbbing legs and the burning sensation caused by her hair being pulled. She was sure he'd pulled handfuls of hair out, but she was too afraid to feel. Her scalp felt as though it was on fire. David had been talking to her while she was picking the dandelion and she'd not been listening to what he said. She should have known better. No one ignored David. It made him angry. How could she have been so stupid? She'd been so carried away with her thoughts she hadn't heard him speak to her. In the past year or so they'd been living together, she'd learned the hard way just how bad David's temper was. Black eyes, broken ribs, chipped teeth and countless bruises had served to remind her to pay attention when David spoke.

When they'd first met, he had been loving and warm, but once she'd moved in with him, she got to know the real David. Instead of leaving him when it first started, she'd believed his promises that it would never happen again and that he loved her. Time and time again, she'd hear him say the same thing, and each time, like a loyal little puppy, she would stay with him. "Love truly is blind," she thought, concluding that she did love David.

She tensed her body, waiting for the next blow,

but it never came. Not daring to look round, she lay motionless and tried to focus her attention on her surroundings. To the right of her, she could see more dandelions and straight ahead was a beautiful cluster of buttercups. She loved buttercups and seeing them brought to mind another game she'd played as a child with her friends. They would sit on the school fields and pick buttercups. It was a well-known belief that you could tell if people liked butter or not by putting the buttercup under their chin and seeing if it reflected yellow. If it did, then they liked butter. If there was no reflection, then it was obvious they didn't. She was roused from her thoughts by a scraping noise behind her and heard David cry out. She was on all fours by now and twisted her head to the side to look over her shoulder, just in time to see David fall to the floor. He landed awkwardly. His leg looked rather crooked underneath him, and he was groaning.

"Don't just sit there staring you stupid bitch. Help

me. I slipped on your shoe, you clumsy cow. I think I've broken my leg and your heel is stuck in my ankle. You useless bitch, get over here and help me up."

As she absorbed the details of the situation, Daisy realised she'd lost a sandal. She hadn't noticed it before. It must've slipped off when David had kicked the back of her legs. Her feet had curled back as she'd fallen. She looked at David, who by now was sweating profusely. His face was contorted with pain, and the colour had drained from it, leaving him very pale. Her gaze travelled down his body to his legs. She could see now that one leg was bent under the other in a very unnatural position and sure enough, right near the ankle bone on the other leg, was her sandal; the three-inch stiletto heel sticking into the skin. There was at least half an inch bedded deep inside, and the wound was bleeding. It looked very nasty and very painful. She continued to stare with her mouth wide open, not knowing whether to help him or walk away and leave him to suffer. David tried to pull himself up and only succeeded in pressing harder on the leg that was bent under him. He screamed so loudly, it shook Daisy into action. She kicked off her remaining sandal and pulled herself up. Her legs hurting as her feet touched the ground and she winced. Ignoring the pain, she made her way over to where David was lying. As she got near him, she noticed tears running down his face. David was crying, something she'd never seen before. For an instant, she felt sorry for him and automatically put her arms out to comfort him.

"This is your fault," he screamed at her. "If you hadn't been playing around with that stupid flower, none of this would've happened."

His voice sounded cracked and broken, but even through his pain, she knew David was trying to make her suffer. That was the last straw for Daisy. She'd had enough. The hurt and the anger she'd suppressed while she'd suffered at David's hands came oozing out, and she screamed, almost hysterically.

"My fault, My fault? How dare you, David. After everything you've done to me. All the beatings and the pain and the countless times you've broken my heart and you try and blame this on me. I won't let you. Not anymore. Not ever again. That's it."

She turned and started to walk away. David yelled after her and she half expected him to run and hit her, but he didn't. He couldn't. This time he was the one hurting, and she was the only one who could help him.

Not expecting Daisy to react that way, David was clearly shocked

"Daisy, no. Don't leave me here like this. Please. I need your help. Okay, you're right. It's my fault. I know it is, and I deserve this, but please don't leave me here on my own. At least get me some help. I'm in a bad way. You know I am."

Hearing the desperation in his voice, Daisy turned around and walked back to him. She saw the relief wash over his face as she approached him.

"Okay, David. I'll help you. I can't risk trying to lift you, but I know you've got your mobile phone in the back pocket of your jeans. I'm going to slide my hand gently in your pocket, but you'll need to twist your body round so I can reach it. Can you do that?"

He nodded and took a deep breath. He raised his body slightly and twisted, as he did so, he squealed. It was obvious he was in a lot of pain and Daisy slid her hand into his pocket as quickly and gently as she could and retrieved his phone. He slumped back down and gulped in air, as he resumed his position again.

"I feel sick Daisy, and dizzy. Do something quickly, please."

Daisy managed to remove her jacket, fold it up and place it under his head, just before he fainted. Slightly relieved that he was temporarily unaware of his pain, she assessed his injuries. It was far worse than she thought. The leg he was lying on was bent backwards and she could see it was twisted badly. The ankle with the shoe embedded looked quite nasty but wasn't bleeding too much. She daren't try and remove the heel from the wound, in case it caused damage to the blood vessels. Quickly, she realised this was an emergency, and she dialled the emergency number and asked for an ambulance. She sounded very calm, considering she was shaking like a leaf and was able to give clear directions. After she'd ensured help was on its way, she sat down besides David to wait for them. By now David was coming round, and she put her hand on his shoulder to reassure him and told him the ambulance was coming.

"Thanks, Daisy," he said. "I'm so sorry. Truly I am, for everything. It won't happen again I swear, and I'll make it up to you. I promise it will never happen again." He started to sob.

"Shh David. Stop it. You always say that, and I always believe you then it happens again and again.

I'm tired of it. I've had enough of your lies David."

"I mean it this time baby. Honestly, I do." He reached out to touch Daisy's cheek and started sobbing uncontrollably.

"You need to stay calm David," she urged him. "Don't talk. Just close your eyes and rest."

She leaned into him and held him as his sobs subsided. He closed his eyes and rested against her. Within minutes, they could hear sirens, and as Daisy looked towards the road, she could see the ambulance turn onto the grass path, followed closely by a Police car. David opened his eyes, and he saw it too.

"Why are the Police here? Did you tell them what I did Daisy?" His voice was full of panic.

"No David. I didn't call the Police. They must have to attend because it's an accident. Don't worry I won't tell them. Calm down."

The ambulance pulled up, and the paramedics ran across to them. They quickly examined David's injuries and gave him something to ease the pain. Two young Policemen joined them, and one asked Daisy how it had happened.

"You have a nasty bruise on your head miss and a bloody lip. Are you alright? Can you tell me how you both got hurt?"

She looked at David, who by now was starting to feel drowsy from the medication he'd been given;

"I bent down to pick dandelions and buttercups and fell over. As I did, I must've kicked my sandal off, and as David came to help me, it hit him on the leg, sticking in his ankle. He slipped and fell hurting his other leg. I realised I mustn't remove the heel from the wound and I rang for help right away."

She saw the relief on David's face as he succumbed to the effect of the painkiller.

"Will he be alright," she asked the paramedics as they lifted him into the ambulance.

"He'll be fine miss. He's got a broken leg and a

possible fracture to his ankle too. He won't be able to walk about for a while, but hopefully, he'll mend okay."

"So he won't be able to chase after me," she thought.

She was asked if she'd like to be taken to the hospital by the Police officers, but she said she'd rather not. When they offered her a lift home, she declined that offer too. She told them she thought she needed the air and would take a steady walk back home. One of the officers remarked that she had no shoes on, but she said she liked to walk through the grass barefoot and she lived close by. He shook his head and started to walk away. He suddenly stopped and turned round.

"I don't suppose you can remember the time the incident happened can you miss. It's not important, but every detail has to be logged. The more information we have, the better."

Daisy bent down to pick up a dandelion and smiled at him as she blew it.

"One o'clock, two o'clock, three o'clock, four," she replied then she turned and walked away.

Good Old Graffiti

My god, we've progressed since we invented the wheel. All this technology available and what do we spend our time doing...writing on our Facebook wall. I'm not saying it's a bad thing mind you. Quite the opposite...I mean remember your school days when graffiti was all over the school walls? I remember the toilets at Upton Middle School...oh, now there's a memory. A visit to those toilets was an adventure. I'm talking about the ones at the entrance closest to the boiler house? Just round the corner was the outside toilets...you know, the scruffy, smelly ones where all the smokers, snoggers and skivers used to go. I never smoked there, and I never skived, but I'll put my hand up and admit to the snogging (sorry, but better to snog than skive hey).

Anyway, it's the indoor toilets I mean, just up past the school hall, near the music store room. The teachers must've thought half the kids in school had weak bladders the amount of time we spent in those toilets reading...yes...reading. You could learn more in a trip to there than you could learn in a whole week at school. I'm not joking. All the latest gossip, news and fight agendas were on those walls. Even poor spelling was corrected...I kid you not. I speak from experience. I remember Mr. Grant, bless him, when I wrote the word 'virgin' in a story we had to write for English. He asked me to read mine out before he'd marked it because he said I had a creative mind. His eyes nearly popped out of his head when I started telling the story about the virgin bride. (I'd heard the title somewhere and thought it sounded good but didn't have a clue what it meant). He must've thought he'd heard me wrong and asked me if I'd gotten the correct spelling.

I said, "Oh yes sir, I checked on the wall when I went to the toilet. You know, the bit where it says Angela Cxxxxx is a virgin. It's definitely right sir because someone had written vergin and someone else had crossed the 'e' out and changed it to an 'i'."

It was too. He couldn't deny I'd got the right spelling. I'm not sure who was the most embarrassed though, him, me or the teacher next door, Molly Cooper, who had to explain to me just what a virgin was. We were never allowed to read our stories out to the class until they'd been marked after that!

Those toilet walls were special though. I swear they were magic. The cleaners would come and scrub off all the writing, and within an hour of them finishing and leaving, more would appear. I never quite figured out how that could happen in such a short time, but believe me, it did. It wasn't just writing that appeared either. Some of the most amazing pictures were drawn, mostly sexual I have to add, but colourful and very creative too. You could say what little we knew about sex was gleaned from those walls. Mind you, some of the positions were beyond my comprehension and thank god body parts weren't drawn to scale, or the people they were supposedly modelled on would be walking round with severe deformities tucked away in their underwear. To this day I swear one of the drawings of a penis looked like a carrot...brings a whole new meaning to 'what's up doc' I can tell you! It's a wonder we weren't traumatised for life.

It wasn't all about sex though. You could learn some Maths there too. There was one piece someone had written about a girl being a 'prossy'...I had no idea what that meant either at the time...I just knew she charged a quid for a feel and she would let you 'do it' for two quid. There were lads in my class who had been trying to scrape up three quid for ages...no prizes for guessing what they were saving for!

Thinking about it now, we could have spent most of our school days in those toilets and still had a full education. English, Art, Maths...all provided while on a visit to spend a penny. You could even go as far as to say Geography and Sex Education too because the images were quite graphic and even addresses and places to go were provided. When girls or boys found out their names and details had been written on the wall, there was plenty of activity and falling out, so I guess that qualifies as the Drama criteria. Oh, those were the days. Who'd have thought a bit of graffiti on a toilet wall could come this far!

No Explanation

Where to begin.

Sitting on the edge of my bed, trying to decide whether I'm still asleep and whether the thing I'm looking at is real or not, isn't the best way to wake up, but it was becoming commonplace for me. If it wasn't a sound that woke me, it would be a sensation of being watched or a feeling that I'd been nudged out of my slumber, by some unseen presence. I wasn't disturbed by it or frightened. Quite the opposite, in fact. I'd become accustomed to it and was used to it, but it wasn't always welcomed, especially when half my night had been spent trying to get to sleep in the first place.

To understand it, you would have to have a sense of spirituality or have a great imagination...I had both, so I guess it was a good starting point for me. It was never a case of things that go bump in the night, more of an expectation of things happening day and night. There was no discrimination of time at all. Things were always happening around me. I had grown up with these experiences and they were nothing out of the ordinary to me. I just accepted them from a young age, as I didn't know any different. It was normal to me. I can't exactly pinpoint precisely when I was first aware that not everybody saw what I saw or heard or sensed, but I do remember my earliest memory of having a 'visitor' as I got used to calling them. I was between the age of three and five years old. I know this because my first memory is of a nun coming and sitting on my bed. Of course, at that age, I wasn't aware it was a nun. It was only later when I saw a lady dressed in the same attire and I asked my mother why that lady was always in those clothes. She explained what she was and described her clothing as a 'sort of a uniform' that she wore for work every day. I still believe to this day that my love for wearing black comes from my experiences with my beautiful lady, who I fondly named Nunny. I recall my mother had two nylon half-slips, one white and one black, and remember sneaking them out of her bedroom drawers and wearing them on my head so I would look like Nunny.

There were many visits from her in the years to follow and she proceeded to bring along a variety of other characters, who I just accepted without question. They never came regularly like Nunny did and some I only ever saw once, but I was never frightened or disturbed. I remember one colourful character in particular. He was an oriental man, who appeared wearing the brightest, most colourful clothing I'd ever seen. He had a strange hat of similar colours and satin pumps. His hair was white, with some grey strands and he had a moustache and long beard, which seemed impeccably groomed. Looking back, I'm tempted to say he was dressed in a decadent fashion, but recalling how he acted and how his personality reached out, I would say his look was more pride than indulgence. He was a doctor or as he described himself, a Master of

Science. His specialty was in many things, from herbs and medicine to worldly knowledge and I was in awe of his whole presence. Thinking about him now, I was fascinated by the shape of his eyes. Not just the shape, but the colour. They seemed almost black they were so dark but so friendly and when he smiled his face took on a whole new look. He came to visit a few times with Nunny, but I never knew his name. I always thought of him as 'the man with the funny clothes' or 'the Doctor Man', and that's how I remember him now. As bold and as colourful as he was, he could never equal my Nunny. His clothes were so bright, and hers were dull and plain, in comparison. His eyes were dark and his skin the colour of old paper that had yellowed over the years, while her eyes were the most incredible blue, which seemed to warm up her pale face. But she had an air about her that seemed majestic. Under her cap, I could see strands of brown hair, neither dark nor light, a kind of chestnut brown, but only the odd strand seemed to escape the immaculate fit of her cap. For all her plainness she was strikingly beautiful and the warmth and the love that she showed towards me are still strong in my heart and my mind today. Nunny was around for a long time, and when she did disappear from my life, it was a while before I realised she was never coming back. I later learned that she was my first guide and that generally, they stay around through one stage of development, only to be replaced by another guide along the way. I have had many characters in and out of my life and all have been there to share my growth, educate and support me during my spiritual journey, but none ever left an impression like Nunny did. She made a home in my heart that will stay with me forever, on this plane and indeed in the next. We will meet again. Of this I'm sure!

Away with the fairies.

Growing up, feeling different and odd, is not a nice feeling for a child, but that's exactly how I felt every day. It wasn't me either who made me feel like that initially, it was others who found the things I said and did hard to accept. It wasn't so bad when I was really small because adults expect toddlers and young children to say strange things and also to have imaginary friends, so for a while, they put my behaviour and questions down to my imagination. Eventually, though, they tired of humouring me and going along with what I was saying and started correcting me. I can't remember how many times I was told to stop daydreaming and making things up or the number of times I'd hear the expression, 'she's away with the fairies', but there were many. At first, it would upset me, and I'd feel hurt and frustrated, sometimes even angry at the way they brushed off my statements or questions, simply because they didn't understand them or didn't have answers. Being a child, I was expected to believe that adults were right and I was wrong. I learned after a while, to just stop telling them things or talking about what I saw and felt. I think I was aged about eight years old when I really started to withdraw into myself and take less notice of what was happening in the real world. My own little world was a much happier place to be anyway. The best times though, were the visits and I soon got into the habit of staying awake most of the night waiting, in excited anticipation, for whoever would come.

It was around the same age that I started seeing things in dreams more clearly. I'd always had vivid dreams, but wouldn't always understand them or remember them. I'd also been suffering from nightmares from being a toddler and some of them were absolutely terrifying. I learned later that the reason they were so frightening is because they were sometimes events and things to come that were so mixed up and confusing, that they filled me with a sense of foreboding. The fear I felt only contributed to my dread of going to sleep and, had it not been for my visitors, I think I would've had some kind of breakdown. The human body and brain need sleep to refresh and recharge, and I was finding it harder and harder to rest either my mind or my body. It wasn't long before my teachers at school started to become concerned that I could hardly stay awake during the day. My mother took me to the doctors, one of many visits that I would reluctantly have to endure. I saw different doctors who advised or prescribed different things.

My parents, especially my mother, were at their wit's end. Because I wasn't sleeping properly, I would be in and out of bed, back and forth to the toilet and most of the time, it was just habitual. I had formed this routine of walking about in the night. They weren't aware that it was my way of keeping my body from sleeping, because by now when I did sleep, there was so much happening in my dreams and my mind. So much information, so many visitors trying to make me understand. I know now that I was wide open for spirit to connect with me, but as a child, I had no idea what was happening. I actually thought I was going mad. If only my parents had believed what I'd been saying and seen through what seemed like the whimsical ramblings of a child. If only I had had the help then from the people I was introduced to later in my life, maybe my childhood wouldn't have been such a painful experience. I think they feared what they didn't understand and that made them anxious and concerned for my wellbeing.

All was not lost though, as my Great Grandmother stepped forward around this time and became the greatest influence I have ever had in my life. I owe so much to her wisdom and experience. She saved my mind and rescued my creativity and imagination. She was my spiritual saviour!

One morning, I was dressed and ready for school as usual. I was happy at school, even though I felt different and I had some friends who I'd known since Nursery, so for a long time, going to school was a pleasure. My parents weren't very well off, in fact, the opposite. My father had a heart condition and was often unwell or unable to do certain types of work, so he and my mother had discussed the idea of him going away to college to try and better his education and get some qualifications. They felt this was the best way forward to help our family. I had a twin sister, Christine and a younger brother Stephen. I had had a younger sister Angela, but sadly, she had died as a baby. Trying to bring three children up on the low income they had was getting to them both and causing them to worry and stress. The additional problems of me being awake most of the night and keeping them awake were only adding further to the situation. They finally decided it was best for us all if dad went down the college route and he had gone to study at The Queens College For The Disabled in Leatherhead, Surrey. It was quite an achievement to get a place there at that time, and he was studying to become a Quantity Surveyor. I didn't know much about colleges and such at that age, but I knew my dad was a very intelligent man and I was very proud that he was my dad.

Because my dad was in higher education and we weren't on much money, we were given a clothing grant and provided with shoes, coats, P.E kit, pumps, underwear, etc. The only drawback being, we had to wear a uniform in a non-uniform school, and we stood out like a sore thumb. Of course, we weren't the only ones in school in that predicament, but everyone knew that we were poor because we wore a uniform. The plus side for me though was that we could have free dinners too, so we always had a good, warm meal and a pudding at school, while some children had packed lunches. We never went hungry. Generally, I loved my school dinners. On this particular day though, I'd gone to school and had started to feel unwell. By lunchtime,

I was feeling really sick and very tired. I felt hot and dizzy and just wanted to go home. The school canteen, a big white stone building, which was as cold inside as it's appearance outside, was separate to the school. As the bell rang and the dinner ladies ordered us to line up for the walk across the path to the canteen, I could feel the knots in my stomach getting more painful and tight and the sicky feeling growing. I could feel a headache starting too, and I couldn't decide if I was hot or cold. I told one of the dinner ladies I didn't feel well and she said I would probably feel better once I'd had some lunch. I knew I wouldn't, and I tried to tell her, but my protests went unheard, and I was ushered into the canteen with the other children. I sat down at the table and tried a sip of water, which had by now been poured into my glass. It made me feel nauseous and I had to struggle not to be sick. I put my hand up and a dinner lady came over. I told her I felt sick and got told to sit quiet and wait for my lunch and that I was probably hungry. I was very quiet and my friends could tell I wasn't feeling well. One of them asked me if I was poorly and I nodded. She put her hand up to tell the dinner lady, but just as she did so, our dinners arrived. One of the dinner ladies put my plated meal down in front of me. Just the smell of it was making me sweat and feel worse. I will remember that meal forever; it was minced beef, mashed potatoes, cabbage, and peas. Had I not been feeling ill I would've gladly tucked in, just leaving the meat untouched. For quite a long time I had gradually stopped enjoying the taste of meat or fish. I don't know why, as I never really analysed why, I just enjoyed it less and less and had started leaving it on my plate. It had caused many arguments at home as my dad would try and make me eat it. I could understand why too, as my parents were struggling to make ends meet and food wasn't to be wasted, but never the less, I just couldn't eat it anymore. The texture just put me right off it, as with fish. On this occasion, it was the pains in my tummy and the feeling that I was going to be sick that was putting me off.

I put my hand up, and the dinner lady who I'd spoken to in the dinner queue came over. I told her what was wrong and before she could say anything, I burst into tears. She put a hand on my head and said I had a temperature, so she eased me out of my chair and proceeded to take me to her supervisor. She suggested I be sent to the Head Mistress as I was clearly unwell. One of my friends, who had by now eaten her lunch and didn't like the pudding on offer, was instructed to go with me to the Head Mistress's office. We walked in silence, me just sniffling the tears away and holding my tummy and when we got to the office, she knocked on the door for me. The Head's secretary shouted for us to go in and we entered the room. For some reason, the secretary had always made me feel uncomfortable and now was no exception. I just wanted out of there. She asked what was wrong and I explained. Unfortunately,

I'd had a run-in with her a few weeks before, and she recognised me. One of my classmates, Stuart, had been playing about with the frogs in the tank in our classroom. He said he'd heard that in France people eat frogs, so he was daring his classmates to put a frog in their mouth. They all refused, but then he asked me, and I wanted to impress him, for no better reason than I liked him and thought he would think I was a good sport if I did it. So I did, only to end up swallowing some of the water from the tank and being sick all over the classroom. I had been sent home in disgrace, but luckily, I never had to tell my mum why. The teacher who had the chore of driving me home had been in a rush to get back to school and so once they'd established that someone was home, they'd simply dropped me off and left me to explain. Of course, being eager not to get into trouble, I'd just said I had been sent home sick. Now, as I stood in that office, looking at her I just knew there was no way she was going to be sympathetic, and she wasn't. She glared at me and reminded me that I had been sent home sick recently, then she told me in no uncertain terms that if I thought putting frogs in my mouth was going to work every time to get me sent home I could think again. I started crying, and I told her I hadn't done anything like that this time and that I was really ill, but she was having none of it and just told me to go to my classroom till the end of lunch time and sit quietly. I tried to explain, but she simply put up her palm and indicated for me to leave the room. I did as I was told and went back to the classroom, but within minutes I was running to the toilets to be sick. Once the vomiting subsided, I felt a little better but was still unwell. I managed to get through the rest of the day, but by the time the school bus had arrived, and I was in the queue to ascend, I was feeling very poorly and now I wanted the toilet badly. After what seemed like an eternity, the bus finally arrived at my stop and I started to walk up the road to my house. By now, I was almost running, the pain was so bad, and the urge to both be sick and use the toilet was overwhelming. I made it to the path and practically fell in the door. In my urgency to get upstairs I had made a mess in my pants and felt dreadfully embarrassed and ashamed, but far worse than that, I knew something was terribly wrong. I just knew. That nagging feeling in my insides was a feeling I'd become familiar with. I learned much later in life that my gut feeling was always right!

At first, it was thought I had a sickness bug and my mum kept saying I would feel better soon. After a few days though, it became quite clear I was getting worse, not better. The doctor was called out after a week. By now I was very dehydrated and was refusing to eat or drink. I would be persuaded to try a sip of this or a spoonful of that, but within half an hour of the substance reaching my stomach, I was either vomiting or would have diarrhoea. I became so weak I had more accidents trying to get to the toilet and was feeling very ashamed that I was dirtying my pants. The reaction from the Doctor was it was a bug and that I was overreacting, that I wasn't as ill as I was making out. He told my mother to continue with the treatment of fluids and small meals. My mother was having none of it, and she sent for my great grandmother, who luckily only lived further up the road from us, in a bungalow across the street. At the time, my mum felt reluctant to bother her, as she had recently lost her husband, my great granddad and was still grieving. However, regardless of her own sorrows, she came rushing over and sat on the edge of the sofa where I was now lying. I was too weak to do anything but lie and sleep, but even my sleep was disturbed by pain and nightmares. She had brought some home-made soup and, as she tried to spoon feed me, with no success, I looked up at her and I asked her if I was going to die. She stroked my forehead and in no uncertain terms, she told me no I wasn't and that the world had other plans for me. I remember thinking how wise she seemed and thought that if she says everything is going to be alright, then I trusted her. I nodded off and awoke to the sound of a man's voice. This was a different doctor. My mum had asked for a second visit. I opened my eyes, and he asked if he could feel my tummy. He felt gently and then looked at my eyes with a thin bright light, then he proceeded to take my temperature. My mum was standing beside him and my great grandma was beside her. She smiled at me reassuringly and I closed my eyes and fell asleep. The next thing I remember is being put in an ambulance and being told that I was a very sick little girl and I was going to hospital to get better. My mum was standing at the ambulance door crying and so was my sister, and I felt very frightened. I noticed as I closed my eyes again, across from me, in the ambulance was Nunny. I felt safe!

Chasing God.

I stayed in hospital for about a fortnight, though I can't remember exactly how long I'd been ill, as I had been ill for quite a while at home before I went into hospital. I remember how weak I was and how at one point I was given oxygen to help me breathe, but once I was put on a drip and given the right medication and started eating and drinking again, I began to feel stronger and get better. I was in an isolation ward, as it turned out I had Gastroenteritis and some kind of virus that was carried by birds. A few days before I had started to feel ill, I had been poking my finger through a cage of my grandma's budgerigar and it had bitten my finger. I remember it had drawn blood and my finger had become swollen and sore. I found out that less than a day after I'd been bitten, the bird had died. It was only after I'd become ill and gone into hospital that the connection was made between the two incidents. It seems I don't have an immunity to the type of virus that these birds can carry and even now, as an adult, I have to be cautious with them.

I missed my family once I was feeling better, especially my mum and although they were allowed to visit, they weren't allowed in the same room with me. They had to sit in a room and talk to me through a glass screen. The one good thing I remember about being ill was my dad had to come home from college and would come to visit me in hospital. During my stay there, my aunt got married and to my surprise, because I had been so ill and I couldn't make it to the wedding, she brought the wedding to the hospital. After the ceremony, a big group of guests, including my aunt, her new husband, my grandma on my dad's side and lots of other family members, all turned up at the hospital to visit me. They brought along lots of food and goodies from the wedding. As they all stood there looking through the glass screen at me, I felt like a very special little girl. I didn't feel odd or different that day, just very, very loved.

The rest of my stay in hospital saw a return of my

'visitors' and probably was when I finally started to understand that, although most people couldn't see them, some people could. In the same ward as myself, a small child was sleeping in a cot across from me. I was no longer in isolation and was allowed to be in a room with other sick children. I think this little girl must have only been two or three years old and she didn't talk much, well not to me anyway, but I saw her and would hear here chattering away to someone, night after night. I never saw who it was, as I wasn't allowed out of bed, my legs were still quite weak, and the lighting was always low at night, but I didn't doubt for one minute that she was talking to someone and they were talking back!

Later hospital restrictions were lifted a little and I was allowed to walk about and exercise my legs. I was told where I could and couldn't go, and most of the time, there was someone with me anyway so I couldn't wander off exploring, but I remember seeing and hearing things that the nurses didn't seem to hear. I was sleeping quite well at night while I was a patient there, maybe it was the medication or just that my body needed the rest, but some memories from then are more like dreams. I do remember thinking about God a lot though.

One of the nurses who had been looking after me had talked about God to me a few times. On one occasion she said, 'Well young lady, you've have been a very lucky little girl. God must have been watching over you, that's for sure.' I was puzzled by what she had said, as I had been told by one of the other nurses that I had gotten better because I was being looked after by a very good doctor and lots of lovely nurses. As far as I was concerned, the medicine and the care I'd had made me better. My curiosity got the better of me.

'I thought the doctors and the nurses made people better and that God lived in the sky.'

She smiled at me and replied, 'You are right in one

way. They gave you what you needed and helped you get better, but if God hadn't been there to help them, you would have been sent to Heaven. He decides if we live or die.'

That confused me further and I asked her why God would send a little girl to Heaven and not save her?

'Does he send some little girls and boys who are naughty to Heaven then and just save the ones he likes best?' I guessed she was struggling for an answer because she sighed heavily and was quiet for a while. Then she spoke.

'Sometimes, God has to decide whether someone is too ill to make better. He doesn't want to make someone better if they are going to suffer for the rest of their lives. Some people are just too sick to fix.'

Her answer was enough for me and I decided not to ask any more questions, but it was on my mind for a long time and I wondered what happened to people who wanted to die. I had daydreams where I would picture God inspecting sick people to decide if he could fix them. Images of broken bodies being fixed came into my head, and I often thought about looking for God and asking him why he had decided my baby sister needed to go to Heaven and my great granddad. It didn't seem fair. I remembered Great Grandma being upset when someone talked about him to her. I was determined that one day I would look for him and ask him.

Soon it was time for me to go home and I remember feeling very upset because I wasn't allowed to take any of the gifts I'd been bought home with me. This was one of the hospitals strict rules to prevent contamination. It was an isolation hospital, so safety and hygiene were strictly adhered to. My dad had bought me a set of small dolls while I was in hospital. They were little rubber dolls all dressed in traditional clothes. I adored them.
I was very distressed at the thought of not being able to take them home with me when I heard a child's voice say 'shove em' in your knickers and no-one will know.' I

looked around the room and couldn't see anyone. Never the less, I knew someone was there, and I was going to do what they said.

I thought it was a great idea, till I tried to get all six dolls in my knickers. It wasn't easy to hide six dolls in your underwear, regardless of how small they were, especially when I was now much thinner so any lumps and bumps would be quite obvious. In the end, I had to settle for just one doll, but at least I got away with it and managed to smuggle it home with me without detection.

I still have that doll. It's clothes somehow disappeared over the years, probably through being dressed and undressed multiple times. As I became an adult, I put it away for safe keeping. It became more than just a doll. Every time I took it out to look at it or show someone, memories came flooding back. Although the circumstances at the time of getting that doll were so painful, they are ones that I will always treasure.

Simply Blue

Pete knocked on the door. It seemed odd to be knocking at the door he'd so often just opened and walked in. He couldn't do that this time, not while he was with his colleague. Today it was a business call and he had to be seen to be doing his job properly. Never the less, he felt very uncomfortable and would've preferred one of the other lads to call rather than himself. He had suggested that to his boss and made the excuse that he had some paperwork that needed completing. His boss told him, in no uncertain terms, that he should've finished any paperwork by now and that if he expected to get out of his duties, he had better think again. He was part of a team and as such, would do his share.

That really annoyed him. When had he ever slacked? When had he ever tried to get out of a job? He was usually the one who did the extra hours to cover for the lads when they didn't fancy it or when they were off sick. In fact, that's how he'd gotten himself into the situation he was in. He was actually covering for Joe, who was off with a broken leg he'd gotten playing for the works football team when this whole thing started. He remembered that day as if it was yesterday and the excitement he'd felt was as fresh today as it had been all those months ago.

He recalled the details;
It had been a fairly hot day in June and just too hot to be in uniform, but as the day went on, he became accustomed to it. He'd only had one call out that day, and it was a quick job that hadn't taken long, so it was a relief when his colleague phoned in and asked him to cover his appointments for him. Joe had been a good friend as well as a work mate and they often covered shifts for each other. On this occasion, Joe had rung him and sounded upset. He'd been playing in a match the day before and had a nasty fall. He'd been up all night with the pain and in the end his girlfriend, Rosie,

had insisted on taking him to hospital. It turned out he'd broken his leg. It looked like he would be off for a while, at least until he could get about properly. He would have to be based in the office for a while and leave the visits to the rest of them. He asked Pete if he'd mind covering his appointments for the day and he'd re-schedule his other visits from his PC at home. He was sorry it was short notice and he'd understand if he couldn't. Pete re-assured him he would gladly cover his appointments and would update him later that night. Secretly, he'd been relieved, "anything to get out of this stuffy office," he thought to himself.

Immediately after, he felt guilty for thinking like that. His best mate was in hospital and obviously worried sick. He could hear it in his voice. He logged onto Joe's computer and typed in the password Joe had given him to access his diary. Two of the appointments had been cancelled. He wasn't sure if Joe had been aware of it, but it didn't matter, he would tell him later. The third appointment though was an interview with a local artist. She was well known in the area for her sketches and drawings and Joe had arranged to meet her with a view to buying some pictures of the local village. Their boss had a promotion coming up and the lads had had a collection for him. Joe thought it would be a good idea to buy a couple of sketches of the area for him. Pete thought it was a great idea and so did the rest of the lads, apart from Rob and Craig from the opposite shift. They weren't too keen and thought he'd appreciate a watch, but everyone gets watches. The lads wanted to do something different for him. He'd been a fair boss, although at times he would say things without thinking and upset the lads. Pete had been on the receiving end a few times too, but it was all part of the job.

He looked at his watch. The appointment was at 2.00pm. He had twenty minutes before he needed to set off. He didn't need to write down the name of the lady, he knew that well enough. He'd often seen photographs of her and knew her name from the write ups he'd read about her. Moira Jackson, local artist. Now he was about to meet her.

He'd arrived at her house early, as he recalled. When he'd knocked, she'd taken a while to answer the door as she had been upstairs. She looked surprised when she opened the door and he introduced himself.

"Oh you're early," she'd told him, "I wasn't expecting you for another ten minutes. Please come in and sit down. Can I offer you a drink?"

As she spoke she smiled, and her face lit up. She had the most incredible eyes. They were the most noticeable thing about her, he'd decided. Although he thought she was stunning, he couldn't help noticing her eyes more than anything else. She gestured to him to come in and he followed her into the living room. His eyes moved down her body, and he watched her hips swing as she walked before him. He suddenly realised what he was doing and he quickly averted his eyes to the sketches on the walls. Her work, he knew that without asking. They all had the same familiar style about them. He knew her work well by now. He'd done his homework and checked out her website. All the drawings she'd ever done were featured on it. He noticed another picture. This time it was a photograph of her and a man. They were holding hands. She noticed him staring at the photograph.

"Me and my husband," she said. "We were on our honeymoon. That's my favourite photograph."

"Very nice," he heard himself say, but that wasn't what he was thinking.

There was something about this woman that made his nerve ends tingle. He'd often seen pictures of her, but seeing her in the flesh, was having a very odd effect on him. He couldn't take his eyes off her. She walked over to the sofa and pointed to one of the chairs.

"Please have a seat," she said smiling. That smile again. It changed her whole expression.

"Thanks," he replied sitting down in the chair nearest to him. "Please, how rude of me, let me introduce myself. I'm Pete Wilde. I have to make apologies for my colleague Joe, Mr. Barnes. He's had a bit of an accident and will be out of action for a while, but he's asked me to take over his appointments for today and I've been updated on the telephone conversation he had with you last week."

The smile disappeared from her face and was replaced with a look of concern.

"I'm so sorry to hear that Mr. Wilde. Is he alright?" she asked, "Nothing serious I hope."

"No, no. Just a broken leg. He did it playing football. I'm sure he'll be fine and I'll pass on your concern. Please call me Pete by the way."

"Ok, Pete I will if you'll call me Moira. Would you like a cup of tea or coffee?" she offered.

"Yes, thanks. That would be lovely. Coffee please, white, no sugar." As he answered her, he caught her looking at him curiously.

"Is there something wrong," he asked nervously.

"Oh no. Sorry, was I staring? I was just thinking you look familiar, but can't recall who you remind me of. Excuse me, I'll go and get you that coffee. While I'm doing that would you like to see the pictures your colleague has chosen? They're in the file on the coffee table. Help yourself. I'll be two minutes." She turned and left the room.

Pete had the strangest feeling she was embarrassed. Mind you, had she seen him looking at her backside earlier, he would have been so he couldn't blame her. He glanced again at the photograph of Moira with her husband and thought what a lucky guy he was. The more he talked to her and watched her, the more he liked her.

"Not healthy son," he said to himself. "Always steer clear of married women, no matter how beautiful."

He bent down and picked up the beige file from the

small table in front of him. Inside, were two drawings, quite rough and heavily marked. If these were the ones Joe had chosen for the boss, then he wasn't sure they'd done the right thing, but then he saw there were two more behind them. They were the same pictures, but sketched lightly and with far more care and detail. These had to be the final pieces. They were wonderful. He liked them straight away. His boss would be very pleased with these.

As he was placing them back in the file, Moira Jackson returned carrying a tray with two mugs of coffee on. She bent down to place the tray on the table and he couldn't help noticing her breasts. She was wearing a low-cut top, and he could see how round and full they were. His heart was racing. He had to stop looking, but it was hard. He hadn't been with a woman since he'd split with Donna, his ex-girlfriend and seeing Moira looking so gorgeous and so perfect, he was beginning to feel aroused. As she stood back up and returned to the sofa, the scent of her perfume touched his nostrils. It was a strong perfume, but pleasant. Probably expensive too. It certainly didn't smell like cheap perfume. It had a lingering smell that was rich and musky. He liked it.

"Well, did you get chance to have a look at the sketches Mr. Wilde, Pete?" she asked him. "The rough drafts are there for you just to see how my drawings develop. I'll be keeping those though. I only ever do one copy of each picture, so I like to keep the drafts for my collection. They will be framed of course before I deliver them in a couple of weeks' time. It's all part of the service and the cost."

She looked straight into Pete's eyes as she spoke to him. His stomach flipped. He told her how pleased he was with the drawings and that he was sure the other lads would be too. He knew Joe had seen them already and that this visit was just a courtesy call. He asked her when had she decided she wanted to be an artist and if it had been hard getting recognised. She told him she'd always loved drawing and when she left school after staying on in the Sixth Form she had wanted to go to Art College, but she couldn't afford to, so she'd taken a job in a factory and saved every penny she could. As soon as she had enough money saved she left the factory and opened her own shop. That's how she'd met her husband, Phil. He had been looking at her work in the window and came into the shop to enquire about it. They'd hit it off right away and he'd asked her out. Soon after, they became a couple. He was a local businessman and had introduced her to the right people. As her work improved, her reputation grew. After a couple of years, Phil asked her to get married and a few years later they had moved back to the area where she was brought up. She wanted to be closer to her parents, who still lived in the area.

She insisted that although Phil had assisted her financially, initially, her success was due to her own hard work. Pete could see she was a very proud woman, who wanted people to know she'd worked hard to get where she was today and that just because she'd married a wealthy businessman, it didn't mean she'd had an easy ride. He could tell she loved her work. Her eyes shone and her skin was glowing. She asked him a few questions about his job and then they were chatting away as if they'd known each other for years.

He suddenly became aware of the time. He'd been there over two hours. She saw him look at his watch.

"Oh I'm sorry," she said. "I've kept you longer than I should have. I get talking and the hours just pass. I'm really sorry."

"No, it's alright, honestly," he quickly answered. "It's been a pleasure. It really has, but I'd better be moving on. I've no more appointments today, so I'll just go back to work and collect my things. I'll ring Joe later tonight and let him know the arrangements. Did you say the pictures will be ready in a fortnight? I'll leave you my number, as Joe will probably still be off work. It's my mobile number. I won't give you works number as the pictures are a surprise and we don't want the boss to find out."

He handed her his business card with his name, email address and mobile number on. She smiled as she took it from him and put it on the arm of the sofa then she said she'd see him to the door and walked in front of him to lead the way. As she passed by him her perfume lingered in the room, and he inhaled it as if to remind him of the visit after he'd left. She had reached the door by now. Opening it, she turned to Pete.

"Thank you, Pete. I've really enjoyed our talk. I work from home in my studio, so I don't get to chat much with people. I love it when I have visitors."

"It's been a pleasure, Moira." Pete said, "Thank you for the coffee and the company. I look forward to hearing from you again."

She leaned forward and shook his hand warmly. He stepped out of the house and she watched him walk up the path. He climbed into the car, pulled his seat belt on and started the engine. As he pulled away, she waved him off. That was his first meeting with Moira Jackson and she had made quite an impression on him.

Back in the office, he'd logged onto his computer and decided to check his emails before he shut it down and left for home. There were the usual polite notices from various institutions and a few other items that didn't really need dealing with right now, but then one email caught his eye. It was from someone called M. L. Jackson. He recognized the name instantly. It had to be her. He didn't know anyone else with that name. He looked at the subject title; Visit. His heart beat faster. It must be her. He opened the email and was pleased to see it was.

He read it to himself;

"Hi Pete, I hope I'm not disturbing you. I just wanted to say thank you again for your visit today. I hope I didn't

cause you any grief at work, keeping you chatting for so long or that I haven't made you late for anything. It was a pleasure talking to you, and if ever you're in the area again, please feel free to call in for a coffee."

She'd ended the email with just Moira. Pete was grinning from ear to ear. He had only been back in the office fifteen minutes and already she'd emailed him. She liked him, he could tell. All sorts of thoughts were racing through his mind, but he reminded himself she was married and that she was probably just being polite. Never the less, he thought he'd better reply;

"Hi Moira, what a lovely surprise. You didn't keep me from anything or make me late, so please don't worry. I had a great afternoon and enjoyed our chat very much. As I recall, I was doing as much talking as you were and the time just flew. You're a lovely lady and make a great cup of coffee. Thanks again. Have a nice evening. Pete."

He sent the email, and just as he was logging off, he saw he had a reply.

"Wow, that was quick," he thought.

He opened the email, and this time it said simply, "You're too nice. x" Again she'd added her name to the bottom, but this time there was a single kiss beside her name. Pete had the definite feeling she was getting the same thoughts about him as he was her, but he couldn't be sure. He couldn't really ask her, could he? He typed a quick reply back saying thank you and that she was quite nice herself. Then he added a kiss to the bottom, just as she had and pressed send. He shut down his computer, collected his things together and left work.

He was thinking about Moira during his drive home. He remembered that he had her number on the sheet with her details on it. That was her home number, he couldn't ring the house unless he had a valid reason. No. That was a bad idea. The best thing he could do was to forget about contacting her again. That would be the sensible thing to do. He needed something to distract him, so he turned on the radio and listened to some music. Five minutes later, he was pulling into his driveway.

As he turned the key in the lock, he found he was smiling to himself. He hadn't felt this good in ages. He got himself a beer from the fridge, switched the TV on and sat down on the sofa. He had a casserole waiting to be warmed up, but for now, he just wanted to sit and go over the day's events in his head. He remembered he'd promised to ring his mate Joe and let him know how the meeting went, so he grabbed the phone and started to dial. The phone had been ringing for a while and he was just about to hang up when he heard Joe saying hello.

"Hi mate," said Pete. "How's the leg? I'm just letting you know everything went well and boy what a babe that Moira is. The pictures are great and they'll be framed and ready for delivery in a fortnight."

He could hear the relief in Joe's voice. He started telling him about his visit, going over the conversation he'd had with the artist. Then he told him the effect she'd had on him and he heard his friend laugh on the other end of the phone.

"Pete, she's married mate. You ought to know better, but I know what you mean. She's a stunner alright. Mind you, don't tell Rosie I said that."

They both laughed, and Pete wished Joe a speedy recovery and promised to keep him updated. He said goodbye and put the phone down. His stomach started rumbling, so he went and put the casserole in the microwave. He couldn't be bothered to turn the oven on. He'd cook it quicker in the microwave. It was becoming a habit of his lately. He was getting lazy.

He sat eating his meal while switching from channel to channel on the TV with the remote. His mind wandered and he found himself thinking of Moira again. What was wrong with him? He'd only known her a few hours.

He started thinking of a way he could see her again. He didn't want to wait two weeks. He decided he'd ring her and offer to collect the pictures himself so she wouldn't have to bother delivering them. When he went to bed, later that night, he'd made up his mind that's what he'd do. He climbed into bed and for the first time in ages, he slept soundly. The next thing he knew, the alarm clock was ringing and it was time to get up.

As soon as he got into work, he picked up the phone and rang Moira Jackson. After exchanging hellos and a few polite words they were soon chatting casually and laughing. By the time he put the phone down he had arranged to collect the pictures himself and promised he'd call round for a coffee before if the opportunity arose.

It never did. For the next two weeks, there was so much work and then, of course, paperwork to follow every visit, or incident. Though thoughts of Moira crossed his mind often, he was so busy he just didn't have a chance to call on her again. They did exchange emails, but although hers were warm and chatty, he had to keep his short and sweet. The boss was constantly in and out with new jobs that had been called in and there was extra work to be done to cover Joe's hours until he could get up and about properly on his crutches. Before he knew it, two weeks had passed and it was time to go and collect the pictures from Moira. She'd sent him an email and told him they were ready when he was, but if he was too busy, they could revert to the original plan, and she could deliver them. He assured her he would be there to collect them and that he was looking forward to meeting her again.

As he left the office, he threw himself a glance in the mirror. He liked how he looked. He wasn't a bad looking guy and he had been told as much on more than one occasion.

He sighed; "If I'm not ready now I never will be," and with that, he walked out of the office with a definite spring in his step.

He reached Moira's place fifteen minutes later and knocked on the door. His heart was pounding as he waited for her to open the door. She didn't take long and he could hear her heels clipping the floor as she reached the front of the house. She opened the door and greeted him with a smile. The smile that he had so often thought of. He smiled back. She invited him in and beckoned him into the living room. It seemed like only yesterday he had been sitting in the chair, looking at the pictures in her file. As he sat down, Moira crossed the room and picked up a small cardboard box. He presumed it contained the pictures. She came across to where he was sitting and handed him the box.

"There you go," she said. "Finished and framed as agreed. Take a look. I'm sure you'll be pleased."

He opened the box and lifted out the first picture. It was wrapped in cellophane. He unwrapped it and held it in front of him. It was fantastic. The detail was amazing. He wrapped it back up and put it on the floor, while he lifted out the second picture. He unwrapped it and looked at it as he had the first one. Again, superb quality. He re-wrapped it and then picked the other up off the floor and placed them both back in the box. When he looked up, Moira was smiling at him.

"Are they alright? The look on your face gave you away. You're pleased with them. I can tell."

"They are perfect," Pete replied. "Absolutely perfect. You have an amazing way of capturing detail. The boss will love them."

"I'm so pleased," she said. "A satisfied customer! Right, can I get you a coffee? Milk no sugar, as I recall," she added grinning.

"No thanks, not today. I've drunk too much already. I really ought to let you get on with your work. I don't want to keep you if you're busy." Even as the words came out, Pete knew he didn't mean them.

He didn't want to leave. He could spend all day in her company. Looking at her and breathing in her perfume. She looked as though she was going to say something, but she didn't. Instead, she just looked at him and then bit her lip. She quickly turned away, but before she did, he noticed the look in her eyes. They looked sad and lost.

"Are you okay Moira," he asked concerned?"

She turned back to look at him, but she didn't answer.

Something about her made his heart race and he could feel his chest rising as his breathing got faster. Suddenly, he had the urge to grab her and kiss her. Before he had time to reason and consider what he was about to do, his arms were around her. Without any resistance, her head tilted back to meet his lips and they were locked in a passionate embrace. The kiss seemed to last forever, and as she pulled away, he grabbed her again and kissed her harder and more passionately than the first one. Her body responded and he felt her go limp in his arms. He cupped her head in his hands and felt her long hair slip between his open fingers. It was heaven. He stopped kissing her and looked into her eyes; "Are you okay?" he asked. "I'm so sorry. I couldn't help myself. You don't know what you've been doing to me since the first time we met. You're all I've thought about."

"Please don't apologise," she said. "I'm glad you kissed me. I'm glad you thought about me. It was the same for me. I don't know why, but since you called that day, I couldn't get you out of my head and when I didn't hear from you I was…well…just simply blue!"

Pete pulled her closer and felt if he held her any tighter he would crush her, but he couldn't stop. It was all too much for both of them. The next thing he knew, they were tearing off each other's clothes and making love on the floor. They were lost in each other and nothing else mattered.

Their passion spent they held each other, kissing and touching as the urges overcame them. An hour passed and although he didn't want to move, Pete knew it would be dangerous to stay where they were. As far as he knew, the front door wasn't locked and her husband could walk in any time and catch them. That's when the full reality of what had just happened hit him. He'd just made love to another man's wife. He looked at Moira. Her hair was ruffled, her cheeks were red and her eyes were shining. She looked beautiful. He bent and kissed her lightly on the lips then told her he thought they ought to get dressed in case anyone came. For a minute she looked sad again, but then she smiled and got up. As he watched her pull on her clothes, he wondered if he'd ever see her do that again or was this just "something that happened."

She left the room and went to the bathroom. Pete grabbed his clothes and got dressed. He wasn't sure what to do. Should he just go and save her the embarrassment of facing him or would that upset her and make her feel used? Before he could make up his mind, he heard her coming down the hall and back into the room. She smiled sweetly and walked across to him. She kissed him.

"Thank you for not sneaking off Pete. It would've made me feel bad. Please don't tell me it was a mistake and it shouldn't have happened. Please don't."

He grabbed her hand and held it. She was trembling.

"I don't regret anything. Life's too short to have regrets, Moira. I couldn't help myself and I'm glad it happened. It was amazing, you're amazing. I don't know what came over me, but I wanted you so bad, and I couldn't help myself. You're so beautiful."

He kissed her forehead and then lightly kissed her on the lips.

"I'd better go now Moira, but I promise I'll be in touch, that's if you want me to. You're a special lady, and I'm so glad Joe couldn't make his appointment that day." He let her hand go and picked up the box with the pictures in. As he went to pass her, she grabbed his hand again; "Pete, I want you to know, there's been no-one else except my husband. Since we married, I've never looked at another man. Please believe me," she implored.

"I believe you, Moira. I do, and I'm so glad. I can't help how you make me feel and I'm so pleased I was the first. That makes me special. You don't know what that means to me," he answered.

He kissed her hand then turned and walked down the hall to the front door. He turned the handle. It was open.

"Bloody hell," he thought. It wasn't locked."

Although he knew they'd taken quite a chance, the thought of how dangerous the situation was also thrilled him and he walked out of the house smiling.

That had been the first time Pete and Moira made love, but not the last. It had been the start of a very passionate affair. Within an hour of leaving her that day, they were exchanging texts. They decided it would be too risky to email. Moira's husband Phil used the PC and she was afraid he would find an email that she'd forgotten to delete. Although they both felt guilty about deceiving Phil, they couldn't control their feelings and met every chance they got. It would've continued like that too if things hadn't changed so drastically.

Now his mind was hurled back to the reality of the situation he was in as he knocked again on the door. He heard the familiar clipping of shoes across the hall and his heart started to race. But this time, through fear, not passion. This time, he wasn't the lover who'd come to replenish their lovemaking. He couldn't hold her and kiss her as they made love. This time he was here as the Policeman. He was in uniform, and it was business not pleasure that brought him to Moira's house today. Terrible business that would break her heart as it was breaking his now. How could he tell her there had been an accident involving her husband? How could he break the news that Phil had been killed in a car accident? His heart was racing, and his head was spinning with both fear and guilt. He, her lover, had to tell her this frightful news, and he knew she would always associate him with her husband's death. Now whenever she thought of Pete and their days and nights of passion, she would blame him and blame herself for Phil's death. She would feel nothing but pain and guilt every time she saw him.

He was just thinking how cruel fate could be and how life can be going so good for you one day, but then it turns on you and bites you the next when the door opened. Moira's face lit up when she saw him, but then she noticed his colleague and her expression changed to one of confusion. He steeled himself for the task ahead. His heart and thoughts belonged to her, his beautiful, passionate Moira, but he had to remember who he was and why he was there. He was in uniform, and whether he liked it or not, it was his duty as a Policeman to deliver this terrible news. He had broken the rules by loving another man's wife and now he had to pay. They had to pay. They were being punished, he was sure of that. It wasn't their fault they'd fallen in love. They couldn't help it. But it didn't matter now, nothing did. Once he'd told her, he knew he'd lose her, and he deserved to. He remembered how she'd told him she had felt the first time they'd met and chatted. She had been so happy and then when he'd left and not been in touch for a while, she'd felt empty and sad. "Simply blue," she'd said to him. "Simply blue!"

Crying Shame

Part One

Katy had just managed to get into her hiding place and squeeze into a comfortable position when she heard the key turn in the lock and the latch slide across the front door. She quietly slid the hook into place and rewarded her fast thinking with a sigh of relief. All she could do now was wait and hope she wouldn't be discovered. If she were found she knew it wouldn't be pleasant! She heard the door click as it closed, and took a deep breath as she heard the footsteps climbing the stairs. As each creak of the stairs got nearer her heart started beating faster. At one point Katy thought it was going to burst out of her chest, and it was so loud she thought the sound would surely betray her hiding place. Amidst the sound of her heart beating in her ears, she heard him shout her name. His voice chilled her, and she felt her body shiver. Her stomach rose into her throat and she thought she was going to be sick or pass out.

It didn't help that she was almost curled up in a ball on the shelf of the airing cupboard. The tank was just below her, and as it was winter and the fire was built up, it was so hot and dry in there. Every part of her body ached with fear and the pain of being confined to such a tiny hiding place. But she had no choice. It was the only place where she knew she would be safe. She was twelve years old. She should be safe in her own home, but she wasn't. Why was she hiding, afraid and trembling? It wasn't right. It wasn't fair. Here she was hiding in a cupboard, frightened for her safety, but it was the only way to stop him.

It was a school day, but Katy had woken up with a sore throat and a temperature again. She'd gone to school the previous day but been sent home ill, so when her mother had seen she wasn't well, she'd kept her home. Katy had begged her to let her go. She didn't want to be at home. She argued that her mother would get into trouble because she wasn't old enough to be left alone and she couldn't afford to have time off work to look after her. Her mother said it would be alright because she would get someone to call in and check on her. She instructed her to go to bed and stay there. Katy really didn't want to stay at home. She had her own reasons. On a different occasion, she'd been at home, and HE'd let himself in. As a family friend, he and his wife often called in to keep an eye on her and her brother and sister, when they were ill. It was because of this that a few days ago she'd had the idea of putting a hook and a catch on the inside of the tank cupboard. That way, she'd have somewhere to hide if she ever needed to. By now she was getting used to planning and preparing ahead, just in case. She'd had no choice. Many of her nights were spent sleepless through either nightmares or busy planning ways to outwit him. She was so pleased she'd had the forethought on this occasion, but as she lay there, hardly daring to breathe, she thought she'd never feel safe again. Silent, salty tears fell down her cheeks, leaving a wet track along the way, and she tried to recall how she'd ended up in this situation. Her mind wandered.

Katy tried to recall when it actually all started. She remembered being about ten years old when she noticed him being a bit too attentive towards her. He always seemed to be looking at her and when she couldn't actually see his eyes on her, she seemed to know he was watching her. She didn't know how. She just sensed it. She'd feel his eyes burning into her back and knew it wasn't good. She was a well-developed child, with very obvious breasts by this time, and her body was getting more shapely by the month. She was maturing physically very quickly and was embarrassed by this unwelcome change in her body. She was a child and wasn't ready for these curves. More importantly, she wasn't prepared for the unwelcome advances that would follow this change. Katy had never had any reason to be uncomfortable near this adult before, but he was beginning to startle her. Her instincts told her to be on her guard and she was careful not to be around him. She also tried to hide her figure under baggy clothes. Not that it made any difference. It was as if once he knew how she was developing, he couldn't keep his eyes off her and then his hands. He would always find some reason to have to brush by her and catch his hand on her or let his body come as close as possible to hers. The hairs would stand up on the back of her neck and his wheezing breath would put the fear of God in her. He made Katy's skin crawl.

Alarm bells were ringing by now, and it didn't matter that his own daughter was her age and that it wasn't right, he seemed to be driven my some sick lust that just pushed him to try a bit harder each time. He would even take chances when family members were around and touch her. Then one day he actually slapped her backside as she passed him in the kitchen. Katy had been petrified, but more frightened that someone had seen and that she'd be blamed. He was very clever. He knew this and the more frightened she became, the more powerful she believed he felt. Gradually, she became a nervous wreck. Having to plan and scheme so that she would never be alone with him or in the same room for too long. His daughter Claire was her best friend, and it was so hard for her to try and prevent her finding out that her dad was a pervert. What he actually was didn't come to light until she was much older. The term Paedophile wasn't around then as it is now. He was a Paedophile though, without a doubt and it would be four long, torturous years before she would shake him off. Oh, he was very careful, choosing his moments with precision. Usually, times when she'd be relaxed and off her guard. One time, for example, was when she was going out for the day with her best friend's family. Katy, sighed heavily as she remembered. She was about eleven years old at the time. Her friend Claire had invited her along on an outing with herself and her family. Katy had only agreed to go because she thought all the family would be going, which included Claire's mother. But she had decided not to go, and so it was just, Katy, Claire, her little sister Debbie and HIM. Katy was very uneasy at first, but when she found out where they were going and that it was a public place, she relaxed and thought HE wouldn't dare try anything there. It was too late to say no anyway. Her parents had made their own arrangements around this trip, and as there was no-one at home, she had no choice but to go. Besides, she thought, it was a lovely day. The sun was shining, and they were going to be eating out. Claire's mum had prepared a lovely picnic and as she and Debbie would be there, Katy thought nothing could go wrong. She thought she would be safe.

They travelled for about thirty minutes in the car until they reached their destination. Everyone picked up something to carry and Katy grabbed Debbie's hand, as well as the blanket they would need to sit on. Claire had insisted on bringing the family dog, so she had it on the leash and was carrying a container of food in the other hand. Her father was carrying everything else, including the flask and bottles of juice. Katy didn't feel threatened as he was too busy trying not to drop things as he locked the car door and followed behind them. She didn't feel he was watching her and felt happy and relaxed. She was just a child and wasn't designed yet for all this responsibility and anxiety, so she just got carried away with the joy of it all. Being with her best friend and her cute little sister, she felt really good.

They all walked up a slope and came to a grassy area. The sun was beating down on them, and it was getting quite warm, so a place was found under a big tree for shade. Everything was going so well. Everyone was hungry, so they decided they would eat first. Claire and Katy spread the blanket out and while her father went for a quick walk with the dog and her sister, they set out the picnic. Laughing and giggling as they did so. As they were at the top of a slope, they had a competition to see who could roll the furthest distance. Claire won the first time, but Katy beat her the second and third time. The two girls spotted the others making their way over to them, so they went back up the slope and sat down ready to eat. It was very warm and they were grateful for the shade of the tree. Katy remembered HIM saying it was an oak tree and that it was very old. To be honest, she wasn't really taking much notice of what he was saying as she was helping Debbie peel the skin on her banana. She was a sweet little thing with beautiful blue eyes and Katy was very fond of her. She didn't hear the rest of the conversation after that either, as she was too busy daydreaming. She had seen a rabbit nearby and was mesmerised as she watched it. As she drifted back to reality, she saw her friend and her sister walking away, into the woods. Katy shouted to Claire and asked where they were going, but she must not have heard her because she didn't reply. Instinctively,

Katy jumped up to follow them, but as she did so, she was pulled back by Claire's father. She was on her feet by now and he was standing, half bent, looking down at her. He had hold of her arm, and his grip was like a vice. Immediately, Katy knew she was in trouble, and her stomach lurched.

She could tell by the look in his eyes that he was going to do something. He put his hand on her shoulder, and she could feel he was trembling. She didn't know what he was going to do and tried to pull away, but his grip on her was too strong. She tried to look towards the direction she'd seen Claire and Debbie go, but he grabbed her head and pulled her face towards him. Katy had to look into those steely eyes and as she did so, he bent his head further and kissed her. First just a touch on the lips, but then, as if driven by some warped desire, he tried to kiss her harder and grabbed her. She was shocked and repulsed and terrified all at the same time, but worse than that, she felt dirty and bad. She knew it was wrong what he'd done and she knew it wasn't going to stop. If he'd risk that in a place like this, with the threat of his own daughter appearing anytime, he would risk anything. That was when Katy realised how dangerous he really was. She started shaking, and her lip was quivering. She tried pulling away, and his grip tightened even more. He got angry at first, and then he smirked. It was a sick smile that she would never forget. He said that no matter how much she pretended she didn't like it and didn't want him to do it, he knew she enjoyed it and that it was all part of growing up. He told her not to fight it and just relax. He let go of her arm, and by now her eyes were brimming with tears. Katy put her head down, ashamed, yet she'd done nothing wrong. She backed away from him, and as she did so, he looked alarmed. She thought he'd realised what he'd done and was sorry, but it wasn't that at all. He'd spotted Claire coming out of the woods. He told Katy that if she said anything to Claire about what he'd done, he would blame her and say she was lying and fantasising. He said if she valued his daughter's friendship she would keep quiet.

"That's what a true friend would do," he said.

Katy didn't want to upset him and make him angry, so she wiped away her tears with the back of her hand and set off running towards Claire and Debbie. Claire noticed her eyes were wet and asked if she'd been crying, but Katy assured her it was just the sun making her eyes water. Claire laughed at her and told her she would be no good abroad, then raced up the slope to where her father was.

He was lying on the grass now as if nothing had happened and pretended he'd been asleep. Katy found out later that Claire had been sent to look for mushrooms as her father told her he'd seen some on his walk earlier. She loved mushrooms, especially for breakfast and he'd promised her a full cooked breakfast, with bacon and the full works next morning if she went and collected them herself. He'd told her to take Debbie with her, but leave Katy where she was because he thought she looked tired. Katy had been too busy daydreaming and hadn't heard the conversation. He'd caught her when she least expected it. She swore to herself she wouldn't let it happen again, but it wouldn't be that easy!

Now, here she was, hiding in the cupboard, having to protect herself from his sick, perverse grasp. She heard him walk into the bedroom, her bedroom. Again, he called her name, but this time she heard him smirk as he did so. The image of his sick smile crossed her mind and she shivered involuntarily. She wanted to scream and shout but knew she couldn't. She mustn't. She had to remain as quiet and still as she could, or he would find her, and he was no longer satisfied by a forced kiss or a sly touch. He knew Katy wouldn't risk telling her parents. They were friends, and she was frightened that if her parents found out, her dad would kill him and go to prison. HE'd made sure he planted that idea in her head too so that she'd be too scared to tell. That's what they do, you see, Paedophiles. They make you believe if they get caught it's your fault and that you'll lose everything. Your family, your friends, your dignity. Katy knew how far he intended to go if he got the chance. He'd indicated as much and warned her that he was tired of waiting and wanted to show her how much he liked her. She was only twelve years old, but she knew what he was talking about. She knew what he wanted from her. He'd told her enough times and even tried to show her pictures once, but she'd refused to look and managed to get away. She'd been lucky so far because he hadn't had the opportunity to keep her long enough or in a situation where he wouldn't be seen or disturbed by anyone. But Katy knew that if he got his hands on her today, with no-one to stop him or help her, he would hurt her. She was prepared to do anything, even risk suffocating in this small, airless cupboard, to stop him.

He shouted her name again, this time angrily and she heard him leave the room. She heard his footsteps pass by her, by the cupboard as he went into her parents' bedroom and then her brothers. He was wheezing by now, and she heard him breathing close by. He was right outside the cupboard. He moved again, and Katy heard his footsteps as he crossed the landing. By now he was near the bathroom, and she heard him swear as he opened the door and saw she wasn't there. He must've pushed open the toilet door because Katy heard it bang against the wall. It always did that if you pushed it too hard. Her dad had once grumbled because it had left a dint in the wall. She was hoping and praying in her mind that he'd just leave at this point, and she would've given anything to be able to uncurl her aching body and climb out of her hiding place. She listened for any sound, but couldn't hear anything except her heart beating. It was so loud, she was sure he'd hear it. Suddenly, Katy heard him come back across the landing

"Oh God," she thought, "He knows I'm here."

He stopped right outside the cupboard, and she heard the handle turn. She couldn't see it move as it was too dark. In her imagination though, she saw it move and open, and she was waiting for him to grab her. But he didn't. He couldn't open it. He knew she was in there though, and he pulled at it and banged, but he couldn't get the door open. Katy was too frightened to be grateful and was holding her breath so he wouldn't hear her breathe. He stopped banging and she heard him saying something quietly, but couldn't hear what he said. Then she heard him move away from the door. She thought he was going to kick it down or get something to force it open, but he didn't. She was shocked but immensely relieved to hear his footsteps disappearing over the landing to the stairs, then, she heard the stairs creak as he descended them. For a minute she was going to open the door and climb out. Her body ached so much and she could hardly breathe, but something stopped her. Her gut instincts were telling her to stay put. It wasn't safe. He was tricking her, waiting downstairs for her to come out, then he would race up and catch her. Katy wasn't in any state to put up a fight. She was too scared and too stiff.

"No. I must wait a while longer and see what happens," she thought to herself, so she didn't move.

As much as she hurt and was struggling to breathe, she stayed where she was. By now, she was so tired and her body was so hot and dry. After what seemed like hours she must've fallen asleep because the next thing she remembered was the front door banging shut. At first, she thought it was HIM leaving or pretending to, but then she heard her sister singing and realised it must be after three o'clock. She knew she'd been asleep for quite a while. Either that or she'd fainted, but she knew that when you faint it's not for long, so she thought she must've just fallen asleep. Her fingers ached, but she managed to unhook the lock and open the door. The lock had saved her. Katy was exhausted, but euphoric. She'd outwitted him. She knew if she'd done it once, she could do it again and again, and for the first time in two long years of playing cat and mouse, she felt as though she might actually be able to keep him at bay. But for how long? She didn't know. She couldn't think straight. Katy knew that sooner or later she had to get help or he would win, but right now all she wanted was to enjoy her victory and have a cold drink. She would think about that later when she felt strong enough!

Part Two

After the incident of hiding in the tank cupboard, it was a few weeks before she had cause to worry again. She was feeling particularly pleased with herself that she'd managed to avoid HIM and still managed to spend time with her friend Claire. Katy loved her company. They were really close and did everything together as much as they could. They were like sisters, and because their parents were close friends too, there weren't many times when she had to be near Claire's father without her parents being present. He tried often enough, but she was always a step ahead and would stay as close to the doorway as possible so as to ensure a hasty retreat if necessary.

One day in Summer, Claire asked Katy to sleep at her house. Claire had slept at her house for the last two weekends and she'd made excuses not to stay at hers. On this occasion, she asked Katy to stay over while her mother was in the room and her mother answered for her.

"Of course she will love," her mum said. "It'll be company for you, and I know Debbie loves her staying. I'll get you all some goodies to share and it'll be fun."

Before Katy had a chance to say anything, her mum shot her a glance that said she'd do as she was told. Her mum was very fond of Claire and Katy knew she didn't like to hurt her feelings. She had no choice. Whether she liked it or not, she was going to Claire's house. Her mum arranged for her dad to drop her off there later that evening and the girls set about planning what they would do. Katy was anxious, but knowing that Claire's mum would be there too, she allowed herself to relax and forget about her worries. Claire had dinner with them and then she had to go and visit her grandma. She invited Katy, but she thought it would be better to stay and get her room tidied before she went to hers for the night, so they said their goodbyes and she left. Katy's bedroom wasn't that untidy, but she knew her dad would give her a hard time if it wasn't done properly. After she was sure her bedroom was up to her father's standard, she packed her pyjamas and other things ready to stay at Claire's.

She was sat watching TV with her sister and brother and her mum, when her father came in from outside.

He'd been cleaning the car and checking the air in his tyres. He popped his head round the door and said, "Hey trouble, are you ready to go, cos' boy are we ready to get rid of you."

Katy knew he was teasing, but shot him a disapproving glance anyway, just to go along with him. He grinned and went into the kitchen. She went up to her room and got her stuff and then, after saying bye to her mum and family, went out to the car where her dad was already waiting. On the way to Claire's house, he was telling her what he was going to watch on TV later. Katy teased him and said, "You are if they let you," meaning her mum, brother, and sister.

He grinned and said, "I'm the boss. Don't you worry about that."

"Yeah right," she giggled.

Her mother was the boss in their house, and he knew it. Katy loved her dad and her mum equally, but she always wanted to make her dad proud of her. Her brother was always his special one, and Katy and her sister always felt they were second best to him.

They'd reached her friend's house, and as she got out of the car, her father was already indicating to pull out.

"You're not coming in then?" she asked.

"Not got time love," he replied. "You have a good time, but behave.

With that, he started to drive off. As he did so, he shouted, "No booze and no boys," and grinned.

Katy just pulled a face after him and watched him disappear down the road. For some reason, she felt very alone. She was soon distracted by Debbie running out of the door dressed in a pair of satin Chinese style pyjamas. She came flying down the path shouting, "Look. Look what grandma got me. Aren't they pretty." She was really excited.

Claire followed closely wrapped in a beautiful kimono style dressing gown.

"Wow," Katy exclaimed. "They're gorgeous. You're really lucky. My grandma never gets me anything. I'm lucky to get a birthday card off her."

She didn't need to say anything else. Claire knew she didn't get much.

"You can have my old one. I don't need it now I've got this." She was so generous.

"It's okay, "Katy replied. "You don't have to give me it."

"Well I can't wear two at once can I," she said, "So you might as well have it. It'll only get given to someone down the road. I'd rather you had it than anyone else."

Katy didn't argue. She was happy to have it. She didn't care if it was Claire's 'cast offs.' She was her best friend and they were always sharing things. Claire grabbed Katy's bag and Debbie grabbed her hand, dragging her up the path and into the house. Like all young girls who have sleepovers, they were giddy and excited and happy. They went straight upstairs to Claire's bedroom and put her record player on. Soon they were lost in a fantasy world with David Essex and The Osmonds.

After they'd unpacked Katy's things and decided what they wanted for supper, they went downstairs. Claire's mum had heated the water up so they could have a bath. She went first, and Katy sat in the living room with Debbie and her mum. HE was out. She didn't ask where he was. She wasn't interested.

Although Claire and her family had more money than Katy's family had, their house was smaller and their bathroom was downstairs in a room just off the kitchen. Because it was such a small room, they had a folding door on the bathroom. This was to make more room in the bathroom without the door taking up space when open. In her innocence, Katy never even thought about how easy it would be to go in the bathroom while someone was in the bath. The door had no lock on it and she hadn't even noticed. When Claire had finished, and it was her turn to go in the bath, Katy was looking forward to the soak. She poured some bath foam in and let the bath fill up while she got undressed. There was a chair in the bathroom to put clothes on, but there wasn't much room for anything else and she could see the practicality of the folding door.

"Good idea," She thought to herself.

Once she'd undressed, Katy climbed into the hot bath and lay back as far as she could. It felt lovely, and she was quite relaxed. Even when she heard voices in the living room and realised HE was back home, she wasn't alarmed. Claire and her mum and sister were there, so she felt quite safe. Then Katy heard the front door slam shut and she thought Claire's dad must've gone out again.

She noticed Debbie's doll on the side of the bath. It had no clothes on and its hair was a mess, so Katy decided to tidy it up for her. She was busy plaiting the long brown hair, when a voice piped up, "She's got a right pair of breasts, hasn't she? And so have you."

Horrified, she looked up to see Claire's father standing in the doorway. She was terrified and embarrassed. She grabbed her towel and pulled it towards her. He leaned forward and, while trying to grab it, said, "I've seen them now. Don't be shy. They're nice. Coming on nicely and you should be proud of them."

Katy tugged at the towel and managed to win it. She was just about to scream when he smiled and spoke, "They're out at the ice cream van," he sniggered. "I can see them through the window from here. We're okay. As soon as they come towards the house, I'll nip back in the room."

He said it as if she was pleased he was in the bathroom with her. As if she wanted him to look at her.

"Go away," Katy yelled. "I'll tell them."

He glared at her.

"No you won't, and you know it," he said. "You made me like this. Teasing me and not letting me touch. You know, you want it, and I'm going to make sure you get it. Maybe not today, but it'll happen."

"Want what? I don't want anything. Please leave me alone. I'll tell. I swear I will." she said.

She wanted to cry but daren't. She didn't know if they'd believe her. She hadn't teased him. She knew she hadn't, but it was her word against his and he was an adult. They wouldn't believe her. He had a sick smirk on his face. At that moment he realised what was going through Katy's head and he just turned round to go back into the other room. He threw her a backward glance as he left the room and she sank down as far in the bath as she could, trying to wash away the horror of what had just happened.

She managed to gather her wits about her and climbed out of the bath. She closed the door and as she did so, she realised there was no way he could've seen through the living room window. It was impossible. The door leading to the living room was across from the bathroom. He'd taken a big chance by doing what he did and he must've known that. Katy didn't understand why he'd take such a risk, but she also realised that he wasn't normal. He was sick and sooner or later he was going to hurt her if she wasn't careful. She knew she would never be safe until he got what he wanted and even then, it wouldn't be enough. While Katy was thinking these thoughts, she dried herself and put her pyjamas on. Her mother was always telling her and her sister not to sleep in pants. She said it wasn't healthy. Tonight though, Katy made sure she kept her's on under her pyjamas. She wasn't sure why. Instinct, she supposed. She wrapped the old dressing-gown round her that Claire had given her and tied the belt. Katy felt safe somehow knowing that it had been Claire's. Maybe it would remind him of his daughter and keep him at bay. When she went through to the living room, it was getting dark outside, so Claire's mum got up and closed the curtains. They were all settled in the living room watching TV. Katy had managed not to have any eye contact with Claire's dad and he seemed engrossed in the programme on TV. She had no idea what they watched that night. Her mind was busy with other matters. Like how to deal with this terrible secret. The phone rang, making her jump. Claire answered it

"It's for you mum. It's work." She handed the receiver to her mum and sat back down.

She started chatting to her dad about the programme. Katy was listening to Claire's mum on the phone. The hairs on the back of her neck stood to attention as she heard her say, "What now, at this time? Can't you get anyone else to cover? It's not my turn. Well okay then, but I'm not happy about it. Especially nights. It's a good job, my husband is here, or I wouldn't have been able to. I'll be through in an hour."

Katy could feel the fear rising inside her as the reality of the conversation hit her. Claire's mum was going to work. Tonight. She couldn't. She mustn't. Katy didn't want her to. Not with him here. Not alone. All these thoughts were racing through her mind, and she was numb with horror. She saw Claire's mother replace the receiver and shook her head.

"They want me to work tonight. One of the staff has been taken to hospital and they've got no cover. I'll do it because it's extra money, but I'm not pleased."

She looked at her husband as she spoke. Katy followed her look and saw him pull a face.

"Oh dear and we've got company staying too. Never mind. She's in good hands."

Then he looked at Katy and smiled.

"Don't worry love," he said to her, "You'll be just fine."

An icy fear gripped Katy, and she shivered

"Are you cold, love?" Said Claire's mum. "You shouldn't be. It's warm tonight. Hope you're not getting a chill."

"She stayed too long in the bath," Claire said to her mum. "Bet the water was freezing when she got out."

She jumped up off the sofa and grabbed Katy's arm, pulling her up.

"Come on. We'll go upstairs and talk in bed."

They said goodnight to Claire's parents and went upstairs. Debbie was already in bed by this time, and Katy could hear her softly snoring in the next room. As they sat down on the bed, she had an idea.

"Claire," she said, "Would you mind if I slept next to the wall. It's just that I get a bit restless sometimes, and if I lie near the wall, it stops me wriggling about so much."

Claire looked at Katy with an odd expression on her face.

"You've never said anything before. I know what's wrong with you. You don't have to pretend. I'm your friend remember. You've been acting funny all night.

Don't think I haven't noticed."

Katy's heart missed a beat. She knew. Katy was both relieved and frightened at the same time. What if she didn't believe her? What if she took her dad's side?

"You're scared of the dark," Claire teased gently. "It's ok," she added. "I won't tell anyone. Of course, you can sleep near the wall."

Katy didn't reply. She couldn't. What could she have said? She took the kimono off and slid over to the wall. She snuggled down and tried to calm her nerves. She had a feeling it was going to be a sleepless night. How could she even think about sleeping? What if HE came in and did something. But then Katy remembered where she was and who she was with. He wouldn't dare do anything while she was in the same room as his own daughter. In the same bed even. She smiled to herself.

They'd been in bed about an hour, both wide awake and giggling when there was a knock at the door. It was Claire's dad.

"You two okay," he asked.

"Course we are dad. We're just going to watch a bit more TV then we're going to sleep aren't we?"

She looked at Katy and winked. Katy nodded back.

"I'm just making some hot chocolate. We've loads of milk, and it needs using up. Would you like some," he asked." It'll help you sleep."

"Ooh, yes please dad," Claire replied. "Do you want us to come and make our own?"

"Don't be daft," he replied. "You two carry on watching TV. I'll make you some and bring it up."

He went downstairs and returned about fifteen minutes later with two steaming hot mugs and a small plate of chocolate digestives.

"Get that lot down you," he ordered, "then let's have you both to sleep. It's getting late."

They ate the biscuits as they talked and drank the chocolate. It was lovely and sweet, and they drank every last drop. The girls talked for a little while longer, but then, surprisingly, Katy started to feel tired. Claire was yawning too, and so they said goodnight and settled down to sleep. Katy was amazed at how tired she was. She didn't really have time to think about what had happened earlier. Within minutes of the light going out, she was asleep.

She drifted in and out of dreams. One was quite disturbing. She felt like she was floating through the air. Then she began to dream she was being carried. One minute she was dreaming she was at home in her own bed, then she dreamed she was in Claire's bed. Next, she dreamed she was in Claire's father's bed, and he was grinning at her. She was trying to move, but her body felt heavy and she was paralysed. It was so frightening, and she felt so helpless. Katy woke up with a start. She looked round the room frantically and then realised she was still in Claire's bed. Claire was fast asleep beside her. She allowed herself to drift back off to sleep. The next thing she knew, it was morning and the sun was creeping in through the crack in the curtains. She could hear Claire snoring. She was still asleep. Katy was just going to go back to sleep herself, when she realised something that terrified her. She was on the wrong side of the bed. Claire was next to the wall and she was on Claire's side. She remembered her restless night and those dreams. Panic struck and she could feel her stomach contents rising into her throat. Her heart was racing, and she wanted to scream, but she didn't, she couldn't. Besides her, Claire was waking up. She wriggled around and then turned to face Katy.

"Morning," she said, "I hope you don't mind, but I woke up cold in the night and had to get out of bed for a jumper. As soon as I moved, you rolled over to my side, and I didn't want to wake you, so I crawled in next to the wall."

Her words were like music to Katy's ears. She felt so relieved. She smiled at Claire, and at that moment, felt she was the dearest thing to her.

"I don't mind at all," Katy told her, "In any case, I didn't have trouble sleeping, so you didn't disturb me."

Then she smiled and thanked her for being her best friend. Claire smiled back and said, "We'll always be friends, won't we? I wish you were my sister. You've always been here for me and we get on so well."

Katy assured her that they would always be friends and nothing would change that. Claire was her best friend and she trusted Katy. They shared all their dreams and secrets and she knew Claire loved her father dearly. How could she hurt her after she'd been so good to her? It crossed Katy's mind that, had she not spared Claire's feelings, her pain and suffering would have ended sooner, but the guilt and the shame would've been too much, so she'd kept quiet. She would remember that conversation many times later, when she thought of the consequences if she ever told anyone about her best friend's father. There was no way out. For now, she was trapped!

Crying Shame...

*Silent tears are the voices
That no-one hears
Caught in the throat of fear
Waiting for release
When it comes
If it comes.*

*Forbidden words
Hidden away
Locked in the vault of guilt and pain
Waiting for release
When it comes
If it comes.*

*Trapped behind a mask of lies
And the ignorance of unseeing eyes
Waiting for release
When it comes
If it comes.*

*A dirty game
A crying shame.*

Over the hill

So when do we actually qualify for the title Over the hill? Is it in our forties, in our fifties, sixties or, as I believe, in our heads. There are so many people deciding for us when we should be old and how we should act, but what has it got to do with anyone else? I mean seriously, why are other people so keen on labelling us. If we don't feel old and we don't act old are we then at risk of being treated with sympathy, as if we're trying to 'stay young', 'mutton dressed as lamb' or 'clinging to our youth' I wonder.

And what do we know about what to wear or what colour or style to have our hair and why do we want to look good, we're 'over the hill' so what does it matter? Well, it matters to me:

I'm in my 50's, not 90's, and I like to look good
I wear makeup and buy pretty clothes
If I want to wear lipstick, I think that I should
And Minx foils on my fingers and toes

I've got all my own teeth, and my hearing is clear
I like Zumba and gym and a dance
I'll try new adventures without any fear
I like movies and love and romance

I can climb up the stairs and keep my house clean
I can always remember my name
I can do my own shopping and still see the price
I'm still me, if you see what I mean

I've got a few grey hairs and some character lines
And a few extra pounds on my hips
But with age comes more wisdom, I think you will find
And if you ask I can give you some tips
So stop labelling and telling us how we should be
And stop telling us how we should act
I refuse to be moulded, I'd rather stay me
I'm different, unique, it's a fact!

Ode to dieting

Oh why oh why did I eat that cake
I knew it was Fat Club next day
I just couldn't resist all that chocolate and cream
And I know that I'm going to pay.
When it's my turn to climb on the dreaded scale
And measure the damage I've done
And the team leader says "you've gained a pound"
Cos' I couldn't say no to that bun.

Oh why oh why did I go to the gym
And work up a sweat for an hour
Then raid the fridge when I got in the house
Instead of going straight in the shower.
Or had a long bath and soaked for a while
And forgotten my urge to pig out
But instead, I had crumpets and cappuccino
No wonder I'm still looking stout.

Oh why oh why can't I just have the power
To say no from time to time
And resist the temptation to eat chocolate and buns
I know that the fault is all mine.
So I'm now on my diet for the umpteenth time
And I'm back at the gym once again
But I wonder at times, is this all for ourselves
Or do we want to look good for the men!

Ode to my left foot

Oh woe is me and my poor left foot
We're stuck in this plaster cast
Already a month has passed us by
I wonder how long this will last

Oh how I feel for my poor big toe
It was taller before it was cut
But now it's much shorter, with no chance to grow
And it looks way too small for my foot

Oh poor big toe, I am sad for your loss
I know once you towered over the rest
Now your role as big toe has been somewhat reduced
And your pain thresh hold put to the test

Fear not poor big toe, for all is not lost
Your recovery may well be slow
But let me assure you, in a matter of weeks
You'll be better and raring to go

Stupid O'clock

It's stupid o'clock and I'm wide awake
What is this all about
I want my bed, I need my rest
I'll regret this later no doubt.

It's stupid o'clock and dark outside
So why am I wide awake?
Listen body clock, this is not my style
You're making a big mistake.

It's stupid o'clock, and I don't need to be up
I just want to go back to sleep
And drift into a happy dream
With my covers all in a heap.

It's stupid o'clock and beyond a joke
This is getting out of hand
I wanted to have a lie in today
This just isn't what I had planned.

It's stupid o'clock and my eyes are tired
Ooh I wonder is that a good sign
Oh yes, I feel sleep grabbing hold of me now
I'm off back to that warm bed of mine!

Tick Tock Mind Clock

Tick tock mind clock
You're keeping me awake
Tick tock mind clock
Be quiet for goodness sake
Tick tock mind clock
My head is in a whirl
Tick tock mind clock
Too many thoughts unfurl
Tick tock mind clock
There simply is no rest
Tick tock mind clock
Four hours sleep at best
Tick tock mind clock
Why can't you let me be
Tick tock mind clock
You'll be the death of me.

A one day pass to heaven

Today I have a one day pass
To visit you my boy
And as my mind travels on the path
My heart is full of joy.
I cannot enter, it's not my time
All I can do is wait
And try to get a glimpse of you
As I stand at Heaven's gate.
I know you're watching for me
And thinking of me too
You know I always visit on this day
To give my love to you.
I cannot travel closer
Than Heaven's gate today
But I know that you are waiting
For the time when I can stay.
For now, I have to be content
To visit you like this
And though it's such a short time
The time spent there is bliss.
It may be all I have for now
This day that's just for you
But till Heaven opens its gates for me
It's all that I can do
My heart is there with you today
My love and thoughts are yours
And one day we'll be together again
When I walk through Heaven's doors.

Melancholy Dream

I dream of silver feathered clouds
Of memories shared and found
I wistful think of beaded light
Pearled rain drops on the ground
Of hugs of satin and touch of silk
The smell of Spring around
With colours pastel bold and bright
And peace of silent sound
Sweet melancholy brings a lull
To calm the beating breast
And slows the breath and fills it full
Before it lays to rest
I dream of love of cotton warmth
That wraps and makes fever melt
And in gold light makes big strides forth
To ease the fear thus felt
In peace, there is a beauty deep
At times it may not seem
Kept safe and warm and held so loved
In my Melancholy Dream

In Nature's Hands

I do despair sometimes you know
That the world has all gone mad
These countries full of sad unrest
And their leaders all turned bad

And hurricanes and flooded lands
With crops and food stocks gone
The millions dead, the broken lives
The damage that's been done

The droughts that leave the land so scorched
And the millions starved to death
When fire and water cross such lands
There's really nothing left

And in the world of stocks and shares
The bankers brought recession
The multitude of society
Driven deep into depression

Is Mother Nature looking on
And watching all we do
Does she stand in judgement over us
And thinking, 'Oh fools you

You had it all in the palm of your hands
There was more than enough to share
But you got greedy, wanted everything
Until there was nothing there'

Are the hurricanes and tidal waves
Nature's way of saying enough
Does she feel the only way to learn
Is to make sure life is tough

Who can blame her, not I for one
We had our chance and blew it
Maybe now it's time to take it back
It was hers before ours, she grew it

She nurtured it and soothed it
Fed and watered it with love
And we came along and trespassed
Even then it was never enough

The more we took, the more we wanted
The more we got we spoiled
Has Nature stepped in before it's too late
And the threat of destruction been foiled

Only time will tell, it's out of our hands
We must wait with baited breath
And see what Nature decides is our fate

A new start, a new life or just death!

The candle of life

I lit a candle for my child
And a cruel wind blew it out
It sent a shiver down my spine
And filled my heart with doubt
What kind of world would give a life
Then cruelly take it back
What sort of wicked hand indeed
That did my heart attack
And break it into pieces many
That I could not repair
And open wounds that never heal
And fester deep despair

So many candles burned so bright
Till such a wind did blow
And killed the light of life that shone
And left the grief we know
Was there a lesson to be learned
By cutting life so short
And need we suffer so much pain
For this lesson to be taught
I think it not, for I have learned
No lesson from such pain
And as for grief it fades a while
But then returns again

I think about that candle bright
And the wind that blew it out
Of how my life was full of pain
And my heart was full of doubt
Then I remember while the candle burned
The flame was large and bright
And made me feel such love and hope
And filled me with delight

Your beauty still remains with me
I picture your face still
Your flame burns deep within my heart

And I know it always will.

Life after death

Do not weep or grieve for me
When I am dead and gone
For though the breath is gone from me
In truth, I still live on.

This is not the end for me
It's just my body that's expired
My soul lives on, believe in me
I'm no longer worn and tired.

I'm free to live a better life
No hate or war or pain
Just love and peace and happiness
And freedom once again.

And if you miss me far too much
And without me you can't cope
Remember that I still live on
In a world of light and hope.

A world so bright and full of joy
Words just cannot describe
And in this place so beautiful
I'm very much alive.

There are no strangers here
And all are kind of heart
Welcoming all with open arms
To help their brand new start.

So wipe those tears away for now
And feel the joy I feel
Take comfort knowing I believe
The 'Afterlife' is real.

The Meaning of Life

Do you ever stop to wonder, about the true meaning of life
Why we have to have a share of both, the goodness and the strife
Is there a pair of imaginary scales, that rely on equal measure
And if the scales are overbalanced, it takes away our treasure
Or maybe when we don't have much, it gives us something back
I often wonder if that's how life is, or just the way the odds are stacked
Do we have any control of what comes around, or is it out of our hands
And is this how the universe keeps ahead of our demands
Does life give a bit and take a bit, until the life scales balance
Or is it all just one big test, to give us more of a challenge
It's hard to tell, I can only guess, but I'd really like to know
Is it all a part of a bigger thing or is this how life must flow
Sometimes it's easier not to think and just fall in step with time
But it would be nice to put to rest, this little muse of mine
So if you have the answer, and you know just what life means
Please point me in the right direction, so I can follow my dreams!

Burlesque

Get into position, head up, then pout
Strike a pose, with leg stretched out
Point the toes, keep your body in line
First left, then right and keep in time

Tick tock eight times, move to the beat
Lightly bouncing with your feet
Move with grace to the front of chair
And lower your derriere gracefully there

With feminine grace, open your legs up wide
Allowing the buttocks to gently slide
Roll your head from left to right
With a smile on your face and your eyes shining bright

With a look that says there's more to come
Close your legs and shuffle back on your bum
Knees together, swing legs to the right
And in true Burlesque style, stand back upright

This is only a taste of the Burlesque dance
Which is cram packed with sexy, with a hint of romance
An art in itself, with an air of intrigue
Guarantees a fab workout of a whole new league

It's fun and it's friendly, it's good for the soul
It's confidence building and makes you feel whole
If you want a great workout, and a firm sexy ass
You cannot go wrong with a Burlesque class

The Last Soldier

I tread this path with caution and I tread this path with fear
And my love for King and country is what has brought me here
Some say this is my duty and it's the job I signed up for
But I'm only here through human kind and their sadistic lust for war.
I want to protect the innocent and help my fellow man
And I'm proud to risk my life for them and do anything I can.
There is no simple answer, no key to close this door
And lock away the pain and fear that walk hand in hand with war.
There is no quick solution and the fighting carries on
And I know I will be needed here, until the monsters are all gone
But I have a dream, as most men do, who have to cross this sand
That war will end and I will be the Last Soldier to walk this land.

Lady of the night!

*The night was cold and a bitter wind blew
In the darkness the old church was just out of view
She waited a moment so her eyes could adapt
Then she followed the road of the route that she'd mapped.*

*It was clear in her head, she knew just where to go
Where she'd be sheltered from the cold, but in a place where she'd show.
She was a regular now and didn't feel so new
She had punters who liked all the things she would do.*

*It wasn't too bad if they paid without moaning
But some would complain, she was sick of their groaning
She'd been warned of the sick ones who pay with their fist
But she needed the money and she knew of the risk.*

*Her job wasn't easy and it was never much fun
She just closed off her mind and was glad when she'd done.
No chance of a boyfriend, who could love her like this
She dreamed to be rescued, love and marriage, what bliss.*

*But it wasn't meant to be, she reminded herself
I'll be worn, I'll be used, I'll be left on the shelf.
She felt sad and a tear welled up in her eye
As the first car slowed down and a punter drove by.*

*He came to a halt, reversed back down the street
He pulled up right beside her, just missing her feet.*

She opened the door with a hand cold as ice
He asked what was on offer and they agreed on the price.

She got into the car, pulled the belt across tight
Then they both sat in silence, and drove off in the night.
They passed the old church that she'd glimpsed once before
And a thought crossed her mind that she'd see it no more.

It was almost a week later when her body was found
Totally naked, her clothes strewn around.
How sad that her poor life had to come to an end
No-one left to mourn her, no family, no friend.

A month later her body was put in the ground
No mourners at her graveside, no crying, no sound.
And the church where she was laid, was the one she had said
She might never return, now she has, but she's dead!

From Kings and Queens

As Kings and Queens of times gone by
Were nurtured to aspire
It was accepted thus should be
Success wouldst they desire.

But t'was not so simple as would seem
To be of such high place
And some would fail to gain their goal
Destined to fall from grace.

Some issue failed to gain their prize
No crown upon their head
A dungeon cold, their fate proclaimed
No morrow for the dead.

Such was life and as such deemed fair
No exception to the rule
And glory was the purse to covet
Not destined for the fool.

With glory came power and ruthlessness
And hatred lived within
Fresh blood flowed free with lawlessness
As did fear and sin.

The executioner did overtime
His blade freshly stained with blood
And anyone's name could be on his list
No matter how bad or good.

So long ago it seems to be
Since the Kings and Queens of old
Ruled in their courts with fear and power
Their favours bought and sold.

With great divide of rich and poor
The suffering was widespread
And for many life was very hard
Full of toil, pain, and dread.

In modern times we're living now
Many things have thus progressed
But though we have much better lives
We live them worn and stressed.

We have more possessions and comforts
No axeman wields our fate
But look around, be honest now
Are we in a better state.

My Forever Friend

Dedicated to my friend Kay

When all is quiet and sunrise sneaks through
When the wind blows in the mountains admiring the view
When all around me is calm and still
I'll hear your voice, I'm sure I will

When daylight springs with sweet birdsong
When it shines its light to make darkness be gone
When echoes of laughter ring through the air
I'll hear you once more and know you are there

When sadness is banished by laughter and love
When the touch of your smile warms my face from above
When memories come flooding to make me feel whole
I'll feel you around me, in my heart and my soul

When all is forgotten and all has been said
When the softest of whispers is heard in my head
When grief feels eternal and life just goes on
I'll love you forever and you'll never be gone.

Sleeping with the light on

Prologue

'On a quiet night, when all is at rest, if you sit and slow your mind, you can almost hear the sound of your own heartbeat. It's at that moment, in that personal state of calm, that you feel the realness of who you are. Your unique blueprint of existence is evident. As you sit in your own vortex of self-being, that is the moment of truth, your moment of recognition.'

These words were planted in my head, and for the life of me, I cannot remember where they came from. Did I read them in a book? Did I hear someone say them? Or are they my very own words and I've just clicked the on switch? I truly don't know. Maybe it's all in my own mind. The mind is such a strange creature you know. You just can't rely on it for too long at a time. One minute it's on your side, urging you with that little voice of encouragement, the next it's cowering in the background of some hidden memories, pretending it's not around and filling you with self-doubt and fear of failure. How often I have had that happen to me, I couldn't say. It's a bit like sitting in the darkness and telling yourself there's nothing to be afraid of, but then the longer you look into that darkness, the more you see or imagine you see. That's the power of the mind. It plants the seeds and before you know it, you have a whole field of horrors growing right under your nose, well, inside your head to be exact, but I won't split hairs. And if you think for too long, anything can happen, anything.

- **End** -